Ghosts, Toast,
❧ and ❧
Other Hazards

Ghosts, Toast,  and Other Hazards

Susan Tan

ROARING BROOK PRESS

NEW YORK

Published by Roaring Brook Press
Roaring Brook Press is a division of Holtzbrinck Publishing Holdings Limited
Partnership
120 Broadway, New York, NY 10271 • mackids.com

Our books may be purchased in bulk for promotional, educational, or business
use. Please contact your local bookseller or the Macmillan Corporate and
Premium Sales Department at (800) 221–7945 ext. 5442 or by email at
MacmillanSpecialMarkets@macmillan.com.

Library of Congress Cataloging-in-Publication Data

Names: Tan, Susan, author.
Title: Ghosts, toast, and other hazards / Susan Tan.
Description: First edition. | New York : Roaring Brook Press, 2023. |
    Audience: Ages 8–12. | Audience: Grades 4–6. | Summary: When her
    stepfather leaves and her family loses their home to fire, twelve-year-old
    Chinese-American Monica, or Mo, struggles with anxiety, but the chance
    to hunt an elephant ghost—and the promise of a new friend—help convince
    her to live a little more dangerously.
Identifiers: LCCN 2022028478 | ISBN 9781250797001 (hardcover)
Subjects: CYAC: Anxiety—Fiction. | Family life—Fiction. | Chinese
    Americans—Fiction. | Ghosts—Fiction. | Elephants—Fiction. | Friendship—
    Fiction. | LCGFT: Ghost stories. | Novels.
Classification: LCC PZ7.1.T37 Gh 2017 | DDC [Fic]—dc23
LC record available at https://lccn.loc.gov/2022028478

First edition, 2023
Book design by Mallory Grigg
Printed in the United States of America by Lakeside Book Company,
Harrisonburg, Virginia

ISBN 978-1-250-79700-1 (hardcover)
10 9 8 7 6 5 4 3 2 1

To Ethan,
Dr. Bullock,
and all the kids who worry
but dance on anyway

CHAPTER 1

TOAST IS A SLIPPERY SLOPE

I'm not afraid of toast.

Just to be clear.

I am afraid of fires, though. Which can be caused by everyday appliances, like toasters.

So toast isn't the problem, but you could say it's the start of a slippery slope.

Since the move, I've been eating oatmeal for breakfast.

A lot more than my breakfast has changed since we lost our house. Don't worry, it's not as dramatic as it sounds. We have a place to live: It's just that now, we live with my great-uncle.

"It's temporary," my mom says, "until we get back on our feet."

But I don't know how she plans to do that, since she spends most of her time either job hunting or in bed with the door closed. And that's not mentioning the stack of bills and letters from lawyers on the kitchen table that she never opens.

So I think we'll be here for a while. Here, somewhere at the opposite end of "on your feet."

But Uncle Ray's house isn't so bad. Like always, I'm making the best of things.

Take our rooms, for example. At our old house, I always had my own bedroom. But now I share with CeCe, in a small room upstairs that used to be Uncle Ray's study. It's a nice room but it's cramped, and when I first walked in and saw the two twin beds with a narrow space between them, I knew I could find a better solution.

Uncle Ray's old study has a long walk-in closet, and our first day here, I claimed it. And no, I don't mean that I put all my stuff in there. I mean I put myself in there. It turned out it was big enough to fit:

1. A twin mattress, if you lay it on the floor,
2. A small bookshelf,
3. A lamp to go on top of said bookshelf.

So, the closet is my bedroom.

It's perfect. CeCe has her bed in the corner, along with a giant basket filled with her stuffed animals. Then there's just enough room for a bureau where my bed would have been, and a big wardrobe from Uncle Ray's basement, which has all the things we would have put in the closet. Meanwhile, I have privacy and a space of my own.

The arrangement is pretty much perfect, or would be, if it wasn't for the whole fire thing. Because if the

2

house burns down at night, will a firefighter really think to look in the closet?

This occurred to me my second night here, and I knew it was something that had to be dealt with. So after some worrying, I came up with a solution. The next day, I took a piece of paper, and wrote:

ATTN Firefighters: There are 4 people in this house (and one annoying Chihuahua). Please rescue us all.

I taped it to the front door until we could get a more permanent sign made, but Mom made me take it down.

So I've taped my note up on the sliding closet door. Also, I sleep with the closet door partially open, so if there's a fire, I'll hopefully hear the commotion and get saved along with everyone else.

I'm still getting used to New Warren, which is our new town. It's a funny mishmash of old (and I mean OLD) and new. Some of the houses date back to before the Revolutionary War. Others are huge and like mansions and all metal and glass. Others, like Uncle Ray's, are just medium or small, scattered in between all the rest.

I think this explains Uncle Ray's street. He lives on a road filled with a neat row of one- and two-story houses, all with little yards. But then, right next to Uncle Ray's house, there's a dead end.

And past that, is the old town junkyard.

Apparently it's old, like old, pre-cars old. And the town just kept filling it with stuff, and then realized how ugly and full it was, so they fenced it off and forgot about it.

You can see it from my bedroom window (or, more accurately, the window to the right of my closet). I can just make it out over the large, red-brown wooden fence. It's so close that the giant oak tree in Uncle Ray's yard stretches out over it, like the branches were curious, and wanted to see what was going on over there.

I think Uncle Ray's so used to it, he almost forgot it was there.

"Oh right, the junkyard," he said when I asked about it. "The town's going to clean it up at some point. This house was A LOT cheaper than other New Warren houses, because of it. Just don't go in, and always wear shoes in the yard, and especially by the fence. People have been using the junkyard since way back in the day, and sometimes the ground shifts. I've found glass, and old nails coming up in the dirt. So shoes, always."

Great, I thought. *Another very safe feature of our new lives.*

But I kept the feeling inside.

Tomorrow is my first day of school, which is another set of worries. It's October, which means I'll stick out—everyone's already gotten to know each other, and the building, and the teachers, and everything. Not to mention the fact that New Warren is a small town, so the other students have probably known each other for *years*, and aren't looking for new friends.

I know how that goes. For most of my life, that was me. Laura and I have been best friends since kindergarten, and nothing, and no one, could change that. That is, until tomorrow, when I start at New Warren Middle School, and she goes back to Ridgemont Intermediary, almost two hours away, in a town where we don't have a house anymore.

Everything is laid out for tomorrow. I have my backpack, my #2 pencils, and a ballpoint pen that I found under Uncle Ray's couch, which he said I could keep.

Uncle Ray isn't like any other relative I have. I'm still trying to figure him out. On the one hand, everything he's doing for us is really nice. I'm guessing most adults wouldn't be totally fine about three new people suddenly moving into their house, especially when one of them doesn't come out of her room a ton, and another is a five-year-old who either talks nonstop, or can be so shy she refuses to say a word depending on her mood. And then, of course, when the third is me, posting signs to firefighters.

But on the other hand, Uncle Ray is a bit . . . strange. He calls himself an "aging Chinese hippie," and his house kind of looks it. It's crammed to the ceilings with random things—old posters, speakers, cookie tins full of guitar picks. He's also obsessed with vegetables, after a recent health scare, so his kitchen is stuffed with weird roots and grains.

I didn't really know Uncle Ray before the move. We'd see him at holidays, or when he drove down for long weekends to stay with Auntie Carol, his older sister. He was friendly but quiet—that relative who you say hi to, who asks about school, and then you go off and leave the adults to talk. Auntie Carol says he's "the black sheep of the family," which makes sense. He has long hair that he wears in a ponytail, and always wears these big thick glasses and T-shirts with band names on them. He traveled around with rock bands and was a sound technician setting up concerts. He ended up developing a new kind of amp and made a lot of money.

Sometimes, he'll just sit in his living room, with his music on for hours, not saying a word, along with his Chihuahua, Serenity, who is the meanest dog I think I've ever met.

So, moving in with him, and trying to fit in three new people around his routines, record collection, and constantly growling Chihuahua, has been . . . interesting.

On the bright side, though, from watching Uncle Ray, I've already decided that I'll also live alone when I'm an adult. I'll live by myself in a big house, just like he does, with my stuff exactly where I want it, like he has with his music things, which take up the entire living room.

I think living alone, you don't get too hung up on rules, or where things should be, or how they should be. That's the only danger: An attitude like that means you can let safety slide. But that's why I'm here.

Case in point: Tonight, before bed, I tiptoed downstairs to do my nightly check.

Lamps unplugged? Check.
Stove off? Check.
Heaters clear of anything flammable? Check.
Toaster unplugged? Check and double check.

I almost didn't notice him sitting there in the dimly lit living room.

Uncle Ray was in his usual spot: in the squashy armchair where he listens to music with big headphones on at night. Serenity was curled up like a small red-brown pillow in Uncle Ray's lap.

Serenity startled us both, letting out a growl when he saw me that I imagine is what a choking T. rex would sound like. He's a tiny dog, but the sounds he makes are LOUD.

"Oh, Mo," Uncle Ray said. He took off his headphones. "Uh, you okay?"

"Yeah, sorry, Uncle Ray," I said sheepishly. "I just wanted to check on a few things. Get some stuff off my mind."

There was an awkward pause.

"Well, want to look in here?" he asked, once he realized it was his turn to say something.

I did, but then I'd have to explain what I was looking for and hear yet another adult give me the "just relax" lecture. Plus, Serenity would definitely make another unholy sound. In fact, as if he read my mind, he looked up, narrowed his eyes, and made a tiny rumbling in his throat, as if daring me to come closer.

"No, that's okay," I said, backing out of the room. "Good night."

"Mmm," he said, nodding as he put his headphones back on.

I tiptoed upstairs quickly and quietly, past my mom's

room, which is downstairs right by the backyard. Part of me hoped she wouldn't hear me, and part of me knew that even if she did, she probably wouldn't get out of bed. A few minutes later, I heard Uncle Ray's footsteps as he walked into the kitchen, the jingling of Serenity's collar following close behind. I hoped Uncle Ray wouldn't get mad about the toaster or lamps.

Or plug them back in.

I was still worrying about it when I fell asleep.

Which was maybe why, suddenly, I was in a field, at nighttime. There was a shadow against the dark sky, it looked like a big boulder in the distance.

It felt very real. The wind blew against my face, the grass rustled in the breeze.

And then, the boulder MOVED. It expanded, it got taller, it was towering over me. I heard a jingle and saw a glint of silver on its neck, like a collar. And then its large bright eyes found me—

My eyes flew open.

I pulled the covers up to my chin.

WHAT A STRANGE DREAM.

That's it, I told myself. *You'll stay up late, after Uncle Ray every night if you have to, to unplug everything.*

The next morning, it took a while to get downstairs. I had to convince CeCe that she could only bring *one* stuffed animal to kindergarten, not every single one she owned. We finally made it downstairs with a lobster named George in hand. I was excited for my cereal (maybe the only non–health food in the house).

But Uncle Ray was standing at the stove when we got down, making himself breakfast.

"Monday is pancake day," he said in place of "Good morning." "Want some?"

He looked so happy about it that I couldn't say no, even though I did NOT want the pancakes he was cooking, which were bright orange and a little lumpy. My best guess was carrots or pumpkin, but I didn't really want to know.

I thought longingly about sugary cereal as I helped CeCe get her juice. Uncle Ray handed us plates of pancake, and nodded to the table as he made his way out the door.

"Well, I do breakfast in the den. But I left some first-day gifts for you," he said.

"Oh, wow," I said, as CeCe ran to her place. "Thank you!" I called after him, as he made his way into the other room.

CeCe unwrapped her gift—a pencil covered in music notes.

At my place, there was a thin, newspaper-wrapped

square. When I unwrapped it, I found a CD, in a clear plastic case, written on in Sharpie. It said:

The BEST music, for when you have a lot on your mind.

And then there were the titles of songs, neatly numbered in order.

Uncle Ray had clearly made this for me last night.

Which was nice of him. And I figured I just wouldn't tell him I didn't have a CD player.

I turned the case over to get it out of the way of CeCe's juice spills. And that's when I found the *real* gift.

On the back of the CD case was a Post-it Note, in Uncle Ray's handwriting. It said:

Living room (if I'm up after you, I'll take care of it):
- *3 lamps*
- *1 sound system: (don't unplug from the power strip—it'll ruin the setup. Just unplug the strip itself)*

I felt better for the first time in days.

I ate Uncle Ray's pancakes despite the suspicious green flecks, told CeCe jokes, and only checked once to make sure Uncle Ray had remembered to turn the stove off.

Before I left, I snapped a photo of CeCe on an old camera I'd found in one of our moving boxes.

"Say 'New kindergarten!'" I said.

She mumbled something that could have been "kindergarten," pressing her face into George's red fuzz.

I gave her a tight hug.

"You're going to love it," I said, straightening George's antennae. "I promise. And when you get home we'll play, and you can tell me all about it!"

She nodded and looked like she was trying to smile, so I decided we were okay.

I gave her one last hug, waved to Mom as she came out of her room bleary-eyed in her oversized pajamas, and hustled out to the street corner.

All the while, Uncle Ray's Post-it Note sat snugly in my pocket.

I put my hand on it and, feeling a little more reassured, boarded the bus.

CHAPTER 2

MIDDLE SCHOOL IS A HEALTH CODE VIOLATION

New Warren Middle School is a long, sprawling brick building, with big windows and views of a meadow and forest behind it.

It's also a little terrifying.

Or maybe it was just the HUGE crowd of students, all walking fast and with purpose, that was terrifying. Because I had zero idea where to go.

Apparently, I'd been mailed a packet with my class schedule and homeroom, but I'd never seen it. I guessed it was lost in Mom's pile of unopened letters.

But luckily the front office was easy to find, even in the stream of people.

A serious-looking man sat behind the desk. He looked so grim and so dour that it was extra strange that he was surrounded by elephants. They were *everywhere*. Elephant figurines, elephant toys, elephant stuffed animals, even those squishy balls you squeeze when you're stressed that were painted with elephant faces.

"New student?" he asked gruffly.

"Uh, yes." I nodded, wondering just how small this town was, if he could tell the new students by sight.

"I'm Mr. Dimare. Head administrator—I know everyone," he said. "Name?"

"Mo Lin."

Mr. Dimare consulted his paper.

"Monica Lin?"

"Yes," I confirmed. "But Mo. Mo Lin."

"Señora Sira's homeroom, Monica," he said, handing me a piece of paper, and a big red folder that said "WELCOME" on it.

"Head upstairs and to the left, down the main hall," he said. "There's your schedule and all the info you'll need. Oh, and welcome to New Warren Middle School," he added, his voice barely changing its tone, like he was reading a weather report. "Go Elephants."

I was confused about the elephant bit, until I joined the mass of students flooding the hall and saw the big, new-looking mural at the foot of the stairs that said: NEW WARREN, HOME OF THE FIGHTING ELEPHANTS. It was a strange mascot, but at least explained Mr. Dimare's office.

I gripped my backpack straps and joined the crowd. The stairwell echoed with loud voices and laughter. But even in the din, as I rounded the first flight, I heard murmurs.

14

"Who is *that*?"

"New kid?"

I put my head down and focused on walking in the right direction.

The sixth-grade hallway had all of our classes except for science, which had its own lab wing. Uncle Ray had mentioned that the middle school was "open plan," and had been built as a kind of educational experiment. I could see what he meant now—the hallway was lined with classrooms, but the classrooms had no doors. Instead, you could look into them through big windows, and wide openings the size of a doorway meant that you could yell across the hallway to another classroom, if you wanted to.

It seemed like it would encourage noise issues. And just be distracting. And it was *very* different from Ridgemont. With no Lauras in sight.

I finally found Señora Sira's class at the end of the sixth-grade hallway. She smiled when she saw me and got up from her desk.

"You must be the new student!" she said. "Welcome, welcome!"

She showed me to a desk at the front, and filled me in on homeroom, and how I'd go there every morning for attendance. She also promised she'd get me a locker assignment that day and offered to hold my coat in her room until I had a place to hang it.

15

She was the first person I saw at the school who I liked. She had a round smiling face, and long wavy hair over skin almost the color of mine. Until I saw her, I hadn't realized how lonely I'd felt in New Warren for someone who looked even a little like me. Señora Sira, I could tell with a glance, was someone you could trust with anything. She was safe.

I couldn't say the same, though, for the rest of the room.

It started at attendance. She read most of the names through without pause, of course—by this time, everyone knew each other.

Then came me.

"And I'm delighted to welcome a new student!" Señora Sira beamed at the class, gesturing my way. "Monica Lin. Please give her a warm New Warren welcome!"

"You can call me Mo," I said after a beat, when a few kids smiled my way. But otherwise, there wasn't much warmth, or welcome, from the other students.

"Mo Lin, huh?" Señora Sira said with a smile. "What a great name."

I risked another glance around the room. A few kids looked tentatively friendly, but more looked at me with a kind of smirk. One boy, behind me, slid his eyelids back with his fingers, into a slant, when Señora Sira wasn't looking. I turned forward quickly. There were no friends here, that was for sure.

CHAPTER 3

CAFETERIA BLUES

There were so many new teachers and units and pieces of paper and permission slips and books put in my hands that it was hard to really get a sense of anyone, or any of my classes that day.

But lunch was the real low point.

It was the moment I'd been dreading. I got my lunch from the food line and took my plastic tray into the crowded cafeteria, tables teeming with sixth graders. Everyone had a group to sit with. If these four walls had been in Ridgemont, I would have had a group too—our table was in the right corner by the far wall.

I'd never thought about how big a room can seem, or how lost you can feel in it, when you don't have anyone to anchor you there. I took a deep breath and waited for someone to wave me over, like in the movies, to give this sea of faces names and direction. But nothing.

So I made the walk down the rows and I found a seat by myself at the back end of one of the long tables.

Hopefully most people wouldn't notice me, and how I was all alone. I took a few bites of my oily grilled cheese and decided to pack lunch from now on.

I looked around: Lunch was forty minutes, and sitting here by myself, it was going to be a long forty minutes. I wondered about CeCe in kindergarten. She's enrolled in an all-day program, which is a lot when you're little, and a big change from the half-day program she was in at Ridgemont. Was she okay? Had she been allowed to keep George during the day? And were the other kids being nice to her? Five-year-olds are usually pretty friendly, but if they were at all related to this middle school crew, we might be in trouble.

I sighed and looked at the clock again. Four minutes had passed. *Great.*

I should have brought a book. And I didn't want to read my new math textbook. So I took out my big red "Welcome" folder.

There was the elephant mascot again. Then a welcome letter from the principal, then the school motto, which I wasn't going to learn, then—

"Whatcha reading?"

A boy set his lunch tray down on the table across from me, though he didn't sit.

"The welcome folder," I said. He had blond hair and

freckles, and wore a T-shirt that said "New Warren Baseball." He looked nice. Maybe this was it—maybe he'd invite me over to his table, and this would be my new group of friends. But then, he spoke.

"Well, welcome to New Warren," he said. "Go Fighting Elephants and all that stuff. I'm Peter, and really, all you need to know is: I run the school."

"I'm Mo," I said, not sure how to respond to the rest of that sentence.

Just then another boy came up behind Peter, tray in hand.

"Peter, come on, let's go sit," he said.

But Peter didn't move just yet.

"Why'd you leave your old school?" he asked. "Did you get kicked out or something?"

"Uh, no," I said. "We just moved. To be with family."

"Oh, so you're boring," he said.

"Dude," his friend said. "You're not funny." He nudged Peter with his tray. "Come on. Let's go eat."

"Wow, sorry," Peter said in a way that was not sorry at all. "I'm just joking."

He went to pick up his tray and then stopped, like something exciting just occurred to him.

"Wait, you're living with family? Do you mean you're living in the old dump with the weird old Asian guy—"

"Peter!" His friend shoved him this time. "YOU CAN'T SAY THAT."

"What?! I just wanted to . . . ugh." Peter grumbled. "Everyone's so sensitive," he said, as he picked up his tray. "Well, later, Momo," he added, with a little salute. Then he breezed off to another table.

The friend gave me an apologetic grimace and followed him.

I turned back to my folder and sighed. It was official.

New Warren Middle School was DEFINITELY not safe.

When the day finally ended, I walked through the door to find my mom on her laptop in the living room, scrolling through job ads.

"Hi Mom," I said, trying not to sound surprised to see her up and dressed.

"Hey, sweetie," she said. I took off my hat and bent over so she could give me a peck on the forehead. "How was it?"

"Okay," I said simply. "How are you?"

"Fine." She tried a smile. "I sent out a few more résumés today."

"Great!" I said.

She couldn't seem to think of anything to say after that, so I excused myself and continued down the hall.

"Mo," Uncle Ray called as I passed his music room. "Your mom says you don't have a CD player!" He sounded genuinely shocked. "Come in, you can listen here on mine. I have it all queued up."

"Uh, okay," I said, feeling like I couldn't say what I really felt, which was "Actually no, thanks, I'd like to go collapse in my closet."

"I have homework, though, so maybe just one song, for now?"

"Perfect." He waved me in impatiently. "One song, to welcome you home."

Uncle Ray beckoned to the squashy armchair next to his. As I stepped into the room, Serenity let out a sound that can only be described as a shriek meets a fire alarm that needs new batteries (so both annoying and terrifying).

"Hush, Serenity!" Uncle Ray said. "Try to live up to your name for once."

"I was wondering about that," I said, as I sat in the squashy chair (which was SUPER comfortable—all of a sudden I understood why Uncle Ray spent all his time in here). "Why did you name him 'Serenity'? Especially because—"

"'Cause he's a monster?" Uncle Ray finished. "Yeah. But once he gets to know you, he can be pretty chill. And I didn't know he'd be like this when I adopted him. I just wanted to name him for one of my values."

"Values?" I asked.

"Yeah," Uncle Ray said. "The things I live by. Peace, love, serenity, equanimity, all that jazz."

"But . . ." I paused for a moment. "Aren't those all different words for the same thing?"

Uncle Ray nodded thoughtfully.

"Deep, Mo," he said.

I wasn't entirely sure what that was, or if it was a good thing.

But Uncle Ray seemed happy about it.

"School okay?" he asked, as he turned on the player.

"Yup," I said.

"You okay?" he asked.

"Yup," I said.

There was a pause.

"Okay . . . well, music time," he said, pressing play.

And I was surprised.

I don't know what I expected.

Uncle Ray is my great-uncle after all, and I don't know much about rock music, and I thought it would be boring somehow, or maybe just random yelling.

Instead, there was a blast of music, upbeat and fast. And then a man's voice, singing loud, but also, almost a story. He was singing about waking up and having nothing to say, and being tired with the way things were. But even with all those feelings, the song was about dancing: "Dancing in the Dark."

Uncle Ray was nodding his head back and forth to the music and mouthing along, and even though I didn't know the words, I found myself wanting to nod along too. (Though I didn't. There are enough ways to embarrass yourself without dancing.)

The music ended, and Uncle Ray paused the player.

"Whatcha think?" he asked.

"I . . . I liked it," I said, barely able to hide how surprised I was. I thought about how endless today had seemed, how not at all fun it had been, and how this music felt like the exact opposite.

"It was so . . . happy," I said. "But, I don't think I get the lyrics. I mean, is he saying he's dancing in the actual dark? Or like he doesn't know what's happening, like that kind of dark?"

"Could be," Uncle Ray said. "Could also be about going on in hard times, or finding joy when you don't know how things are going to turn out."

"I dunno," I said doubtfully. "I don't think I could sound happy about that."

"Ha!" Uncle Ray barked, startling Serenity. "Fair, kid." Uncle Ray went on, "That's Bruce Springsteen. People call him 'the Boss,' and with good reason. He's one of the greats."

"Neat," I said, smiling at him. "Thanks, Uncle Ray."

Uncle Ray smiled back and then nodded a few times at the air, like he wasn't sure what to say next (which I can relate to).

"Well, I guess you have to get to homework," he said finally.

"Yeah," I said. "Well, thanks again. What will you do?"

"Oh, I'm just going to sit here and put on a record," he said.

I got up, and was about to leave, but then turned back. Listening to one song? I get that. But sitting like Uncle Ray does, for hours, listening to whole records?

"What do you do, exactly," I asked, "when you listen to music? I mean, do you just sit here? Doesn't that get boring?"

"Never," he said. "Music brings stuff up, you know?"

I didn't know.

"The music carries me along," he tried to explain. "It takes me places."

"Real places?" I asked.

"Sometimes," he said. "Places I've been. Memories. Feelings. They come back up. It's like the song tells me I'm not alone—that other people have been there too."

"So it's . . . fun?" I settled on.

"It's . . ." He searched for the word. "It's true."

"Oh, uh, I see," I said, more confused than ever. "Well, thanks again. I'll go do homework now."

"Rad!" He grinned and plugged his huge headphones in, so he wouldn't bother us.

As I grabbed an apple from the kitchen, and went to lie on my bed and face homework, I realized that Uncle Ray and I would probably never quite see the world in the same way.

But still—it was nice to share something that was important to him.

And I *had* liked the song. In fact, as I sat and began my homework, I found myself wishing that I could have danced through the day, and shown people like Peter and all those other kids that I didn't care what they thought. Just like Bruce Springsteen.

CeCe came home just a little while later.

"Art was my favorite," she reported right away. "I drew George." We got the picture out, and I told her how I loved how she'd drawn his smile. The full report was promising: Her teacher was nice, one kid had been mean at morning circle, but another had played with her at recess, so it seemed to all balance out.

That night, I had strange dreams. I was in the dark, and someone wanted me to dance, but I didn't know how. But I knew I had to dance, and I didn't want to, and there were eyes looking at me.

The music playing was creepy, like strange, faraway, old-timey music, the kind you'd hear at a carnival in a black-and-white movie.

Just when the dark seemed unbearable, and the eyes were everywhere, a glowing light rolled toward me and the dark disappeared. The music changed, now energetic and fast, and I knew I didn't have to be scared anymore. I reached toward the light. It was a marble. A swirling, luminous blue marble that felt cool in the palm of my hand. I was safe.

Then a scream sounded, and all of a sudden there were blinding orange flames everywhere, and the marble started to dim and go dark . . .

I woke up. My fingers were curled tightly, like my hand was still holding a marble. But I wasn't, of course. It had just been a dream.

Another super-weird dream.

But hey, I reasoned. I was in a new place, sleeping in a literal closet, at a new school that wasn't turning out to be the best. It made sense that I'd have some strange dreams as I got used to things.

Relax, I told myself, as I tried to get back to sleep. *What are a few bad dreams?*

The answer is, it turns out: everything.

CHAPTER 4

GHOSTS AREN'T REAL, SMALL APPLIANCE FIRES ARE

I woke up yawning, not feeling very rested. But still, I was ready.

At lunch I skipped the cafeteria and headed straight for the library. Technically there was no eating allowed there (which I understand, because spilled food attracts mice and other pests), but I figured I'd be careful. And I'd seen other kids there at lunch. New Warren Middle School, I was learning, was pretty lax about these kinds of things.

I'd surprised Uncle Ray in the kitchen that morning. He'd been making coffee and humming to himself, while Serenity snored like a clogged lawn mower from his dog bed.

"Oh, uh, hi," Uncle Ray had said, with an expression that was half-embarrassed, and half like he wished he'd had a little more time to himself.

"Good morning," I'd mumbled. "I'm just making

lunch, but then I'll get out of your way . . ." I went to make a PB and J sandwich, but Uncle Ray surprised me.

"What?!" he said, looking at the ingredients.

"No niece of mine will eat that!" he said, whisking away the jar of peanut butter before I could open it. "Here, let me."

I didn't see exactly what he'd made, and I hadn't recognized half of the vegetables he pulled out. But it was a really nice gesture.

I clutched a paper bag with a lunch from Uncle Ray as I made my way to the back of the library, out of sight of the librarian, and found the perfect table, back where no one could see, in between rows of books.

I settled down with my lunch and examined the sandwich Uncle Ray had packed for me. There was some sort of bean? Pickle? Maybe cheese? I sniffed it, and it smelled okay. I was just about to risk the first bite when—

CLUNK.

I ducked as a book *fell from the sky*, landing just a foot away from me.

I whirled and looked up, ready to take cover if this was an earthquake.

And then I almost screamed. Where the book had been, on a high-up shelf, a FACE was staring down at me.

"Hi." It grinned. "Sorry about that! I'm Nathaniel, what's your name?"

"WHAT ARE YOU DOING UP THERE?!" I jumped up from my seat, just barely remembering to keep my voice down so the librarian didn't hear.

Now I could see him clearly. This boy had *climbed* the stacks—he was standing on the edge of a shelf, three or four rows up on the other side, peering through.

"Get down!" I said. "You almost hit me! That's dangerous! Also, you could fall," I added, though I'll admit I wasn't feeling super worried about *his* safety at that moment.

He climbed down, or more like slid down, taking a giant book with him as he went.

"Trust me," he said. "It would be much more dangerous if I hadn't gone up there. Do you know what this is?"

He came around the shelves and held out the giant book so I could see it.

It was old and covered in dust, and read, in faded grayish letters: *The Art of Exorcism.*

"Uhhhh." I didn't know what to say. What was this book even doing in a middle school library?!

"See, if there's a ghost around, you can't wait," he said, like it was the most obvious, everyday thing. "*That's* dangerous. You have to be prepared. That's how you keep people safe. So I needed this. To study."

"Oookay," I said, searching his face and waiting for him to say "just kidding." But he looked very serious. So serious, I couldn't help myself.

"You know, there's no such thing as ghosts," I said.

"Oh, they're totally real," he said, undeterred. "Just look at our school mascot."

"Our mascot?" It felt like nothing this boy said was making sense.

"Oh, you don't know the story?" He actually clapped his hands in excitement. "Our new mascot is an elephant because an elephant ghost haunts the streets of New Warren at night!" he said. "Isn't that cool?!"

"Wh-what are you talking about?" I asked finally.

"Well, that's what people say. I believe it, of course. Though my dad says it's just part of a new push to make New Warren more exciting and more interesting to tourists. I mean, that's why they changed our mascot, and they might even put up an elephant sculpture somewhere. But yeah, apparently, it's an ancient town legend! It's official!"

What was this place? I wondered if New Warren had a gas leak that no one knew about. Why was everyone here SO WEIRD?

"Has anyone ever actually seen this ghost?" I asked. "Do you have proof?" For a second, I worried I'd really offended him. But he nodded thoughtfully.

"No," he admitted, "but I will someday. I'm going to be a ghost hunter, and I'll show the world ghosts are real. Just give me time."

I didn't know how to respond to a statement like that. So I just said, "Well, that's very interesting. But if you really want something to worry about, it should be fires. Common kitchen appliances, like toasters, are a leading cause of household fires. Anyway, I'm going to go back to my lunch—"

"But the thing with ghosts is that they can literally be anywhere, so they're even more common than toasters," the boy went on, not noticing me edging away. "Besides, my Zayde was a doctor and he was BIG on safety precautions, but he never mentioned toasters. I don't think they're something you have to worry about.

"Also"—he leaned in like he was about to tell a secret—"I even think this library is haunted. I come here every day for lunch, and sometimes, books have moved, and even disappear!"

"It's a school library," I pointed out. "People check out books."

"I dunno." He shook his head. "It's suspicious!"

I was definitely done with this conversation. I had enough things to worry about—I was not about to add made-up fears to the list.

"Okay," I said, in the voice I use with CeCe when

it's *really* time for bed and I'm warning her that this is seriously the last story. "Well, if I see any ghosts, I'll let you know."

I sat back down at the table and picked up my mystery vegetable sandwich like it was the most interesting, delicious thing in the world.

"Oh," he said, finally getting the hint. "Do you want to eat with me? I have a table in the back. I come here a lot."

"Well," I said. "I have some homework to do. New student stuff. But have fun, uh, exorcising!"

"Oh, sure. Thanks." His voice sounded casual, but his face looked disappointed. I tried not to feel bad as he walked away. *I do want friends*, I told myself. *It's just that we would NOT get along.*

I'm only afraid of real things.

Besides, I would NEVER seek out danger, even with something made up like ghosts. That's a pretty obvious rule right there.

But all in all, the day had been fine. I kept my head down and felt like I was getting used to the rhythm of school. And when I got home, there was good news waiting for me.

"Molly asked me on a playdate!" CeCe said, running toward me from the bus and throwing her arms around me. "Can I go can I go can I go?!"

"Of course!" I said, smiling. "That's amazing news!"

And there was more. My mom had been out that day, which was unusual. And when she came back, she was *smiling*.

"I got a job," she announced. "Receptionist at a law firm right in town. The perfect new start."

"YAY!" we all cheered. Without thinking, I ran and hugged her. Her arms came around me, and I realized that it had been ages since she'd hugged me like this—in a happy, protective way, like I'd just done with CeCe.

It was like the thought occurred to us at the same time, and we broke apart.

Nothing could dampen the mood that night, though. And I smiled right along with everyone else, because this was *amazing*. CeCe was happy, and she was making friends at school. And my mom had a *job*, a real live job. I remembered when she'd lost the old one, and how horribly things changed when she did. This was the first step. We were getting on our feet after all.

That night, before bed, Uncle Ray and I sat down for another listen. We seemed to have a little rhythm now.

"How are you doing?" he asked, as he queued the song up.

"Good," I said.

"School okay?"

"Yep," I said.

Then a pause.

"Okay, music time!" Uncle Ray said.

This time it was a song called "You Can't Always Get What You Want" by the Rolling Stones. It felt like the title said it all.

"Whatcha think?" Uncle Ray asked when it was over.

"That was great advice," I said. "I didn't know rock could be so practical."

Because maybe I wasn't going to find friends here in New Warren. I wouldn't get everything I want right in this moment. But I *could* help my family be happy. I could help us get what we needed.

"Cool interpretation, Mo," Uncle Ray said. "Yeah, it's nice to know that even rock stars don't always get what they want, huh? We're all just people, trying to do our best."

"Right!" I said. And we nodded, understanding each other, as the song looped and started again.

For the first night since we moved, I went to bed feeling happy.

I knew everything was going to be okay.

I went to bed in the best mood I'd been in since we'd moved. And it lasted all through the end of the week.

Until I learned about the fire. And saw the ghost.

CHAPTER 5

DIAL *N* FOR NOPE

I kept to myself the rest of that week, finding a good rhythm, getting to know my teachers and eating lunch in the library (though I found a new corner, where I could hide away without having to feel bad when Nathaniel walked by with his lunch).

In math, I managed to partner with someone who wasn't Peter—a girl named Kerissa, who pulled out an Ironheart comic the moment class was over.

"Have you read any Ms. Marvel?" I asked.

"No, not yet. Do you like it?"

"It's AMAZING," I said.

She smiled.

"Thanks, I'll check it out."

So that was one nice, normal interaction at this school.

By Friday afternoon, I actually felt pretty great. I'd done it! My first week, over. And nothing terrible had happened.

My last class let out a little early, and I practically raced to my locker, excited for the weekend. I had a rare few minutes by myself, so I waited in the front hall, looking at the elephant mural.

"Stupid, right, Momo?" a voice said from behind me, making me jump.

I whirled around.

"It's *Mo*, Peter," I said. "And what?"

"The elephant." Peter nodded at the mural. "Our mascot. New this year. It's a joke. If they really wanted to honor our history, it should be barbecued or something."

"What are you talking about?" I asked. I looked at the clock. Five minutes before the bell.

"The elephant in all the town ads. You know the real story, right? It died in a giant fire in a circus tent, in some random field in New Warren. So why would they want it to be our mascot? And if the elephant *is* haunting us, like random people say, then it's just looking for revenge."

Peter's words felt, suddenly, very far away.

A fire, a giant fire. A fire big enough to burn an *elephant*.

The thought squeezed itself into my brain, and it was all I could see.

"Uh, earth to Momo?" Peter said. "You're scared, aren't you?"

His words brought me back.

"No," I said with more snap than I'd meant. "*I don't believe in ghosts.*"

"Well, me neither, I'm not a baby," Peter snapped back, though I swear, for a moment, he looked disappointed. "I just thought you should know the story."

"Well, I do," I said. "And I have to get to the bus."

Peter followed me down the hall.

"You seem upset," he said.

"I'm not," I mumbled.

"You are," he said. He looked behind me, eyes wide. "Ghost!" he yelled.

"Ha ha," I said, pausing to put my coat on.

Peter looked puzzled for a second, and then grinned.

"Giant fire!" he yelled.

"*Stop*," I hissed. "I get it."

"We could add flames to the mascot," Peter said, with an almost gleeful expression. "With no escape—"

"STOP," I said.

"Is everything okay here?" an adult voice cut in.

"Oh. Hi, Ms. Shay," Peter said to a teacher I didn't know. "Yeah, we were just kidding around."

Ms. Shay crossed her arms.

"Mo doesn't look like she's having fun," she said.

"I'm fine," I said quietly. Ms. Shay raised an eyebrow.

"Well, Peter," she said, "I want you to see me Monday in your free period. Come straight to my office.

And, Mo, I'm the sixth-grade guidance counselor, and I've been meaning to check in with you. Why don't you come to my office for lunch on Monday?"

"But . . . ," I said.

"But . . . ," Peter said.

"Monday." Ms. Shay's tone was clear. "Both of you. Now scoot."

Peter and I walked off down the hall, Ms. Shay watching us the whole way.

"Thanks a lot," I muttered, trying to keep all my feelings tamped down so Ms. Shay wouldn't see and find something else to worry about.

"I was just kidding around," Peter muttered back, sounding almost . . . sad? But I wasn't buying it. In fact, I was so angry that my fists curled at my sides, and I wanted to grab him by his coat and shake him. I wanted to yell: "Do you know how much I have to deal with right now?"

But, of course, I didn't say anything.

"You just stay away from me," I said, with more heat than I'd meant. "I don't want to have anything to do with you."

"Jeez fine, sorry," Peter mumbled.

Thankfully, we had to go in different directions just then—Peter to the carpool pickup area, me to my bus.

I watched him go with relief.

I did NOT like that kid.

And on the bus, I told myself that he'd been lying about the fire, a fire so big it could engulf a whole elephant and—no.

I took a deep breath and willed the thought to disappear.

I was so distracted when I got home, though, that when the phone rang, I answered it without checking the number.

"Hey!" Laura said. "How are you?"

"Hi," I said. "Okay. How are you?"

"I'm good!" she said. "The funniest thing happened at school today. I was in the library with Lily, and we were researching our Great Brain, and, uh . . ." She trailed off.

The Great Brain is a big school research project that you do at Ridgemont in teams. She and I had planned to do one together.

"I wish you were here," she said finally.

"Me too," I said.

There was a pause.

"So . . . how is your new school?" she asked.

"It's okay. There are no doors, though."

"Weird!" she said.

We giggled, and for one wonderful moment, there we were. Me and Laura. Best friends.

Then I heard voices in the background.

"Oh, sorry, we have company over," Laura said.

I felt my stomach tie a knot.

"Company. Oh. Is—?"

"No," she said quickly. "I haven't seen him in a few, uh."

"I have to go," I said abruptly.

"Oh," Laura said quietly. She sounded sad. "Okay. Bye."

"Bye," I said.

I hung up the phone and looked at it for a while, like it might sprout teeth.

I missed Laura. But I was also remembering that friendship could be dangerous.

I wished I hadn't answered. And I really wished I hadn't run into Peter.

I couldn't quite shake how I was feeling for the rest of the day. When I went to listen to a song with Uncle Ray that afternoon, he asked our usual: "You okay?" And I meant to say "yes," I really did, but instead I might have said something like:

"WHY DOES EVERYONE ALWAYS ASK ME THAT? YES I'M FINE."

"Okaaay," Uncle Ray said. "Well, uh, song time!"

And then I felt bad, and even the music felt off. Because we listened to "Stand by Me" by Ben E. King, which I've heard before, but never really listened to. And while the general idea of the title is nice, it also starts talking about the sky falling and mountains crumbling, and I just didn't need that in my life.

It was a relief to put CeCe to bed, and to go to sleep. (After my nightly check, of course. I may have done it twice, just to be on the safe side.)

Tomorrow will be better, I told myself. *Forget about the fire.*

And finally, somehow, I fell asleep . . .

. . . and woke up somewhere else.

CHAPTER 6

A DREAM

I was standing at the window of our old house. On the second floor.

That's why it was weird that there were eyes staring through the window.

I wasn't scared, though. In fact, I pushed the window open so I could lean out.

The elephant was beautiful. Her skin was dappled gray, and close up, I could see the details of her face: the expressive wrinkles around her eyes, and the very human curve of her mouth.

And I noticed another funny detail. She had a little silver bell around her neck, dangling from a braided red cord.

It chimed lightly as she rumbled a tentative, shy hello.

"Hi there," I whispered.

Then, because it's a dream, and you can be goofy in a dream, and have perfectly normal and polite conversation with an elephant, I said:

"I'm Mo. Pleased to meet you. What's your name?"

As if in an answer, the elephant reached out with her trunk. My hand met it. I felt her soft, thick skin. Everything about her was huge but gentle.

She placed a beautiful blue marble in my hand, daintily, with the tip of her trunk. It was like a mother giving a baby a gift. She patted my hand affectionately as it closed around the marble.

And then . . .

"Behind you!" I shouted.

The peaceful night shattered as smoke and fire poured from behind her.

She screamed in panic; I screamed for her.

"Run!" I yelled. "Run!"

But she was too scared, and there was smoke everywhere, and I couldn't see anything.

And as the elephant screamed, I heard another voice behind me, a ghostly, lost, familiar voice.

"Mo!" CeCe called, sounding scared and far away. "Mo! Mo!"

When I woke up, I kept my eyes closed for a beat. *It was just a dream*, I told myself. *Just a dream. No more ghost stories, okay* . . .

Then I opened my eyes.

And found that for the first time in four years, I'd sleepwalked.

I was in the hallway, on the second floor of Uncle Ray's house. I'd been lying on the carpeted floor, with a blanket shoved under my head, like a kind of pillow. Above me, the second-story window was open.

And through it, I could see, and smell, a gray, curling plume of smoke.

CHAPTER 7

MARBLES AND MEMORIES

"Something in the junkyard sparked, maybe over-heated in the sun," Uncle Ray said. "Nothing to worry about."

"Does this happen a lot?" my mom asked. She was up early—even she couldn't sleep through the fire trucks that sped by Uncle Ray's house to put out the small fire in the junkyard. "A fluke," they told Uncle Ray.

"No, it doesn't," Uncle Ray said reassuringly. "We've never had a problem before. I guess it just needs to be cleaned out a little. Really, it's not dangerous."

I maybe let out a noise—a squeak? I meant it to be a word, but it had been a weird night. And you know my general feelings about fire.

"What's wrong, Mo?" my mom asked, just as Uncle Ray said, "It's okay, Mo. There haven't been any fires there before this. The fire department is combing through everything now. They'll make sure it's safe," he added.

"Okay," I mumbled.

I didn't answer my mom's question, though, just took a pointed bite of whole-grain cereal.

Her forehead crinkled for a moment in an old, familiar way, but then Uncle Ray said, "Shoot, Carol will be here soon!"

And then we were all caught up in the bustle of getting ready.

Auntie Carol, my great-aunt, is our only other relative who lives in Massachusetts. Auntie Carol and Uncle Ray's oldest brother—my Gung Gung—lives in California.

When we lost our house, Gung Gung and Poh Poh wanted to come help us figure things out. But Poh Poh had just had foot surgery and couldn't fly and needed Gung Gung to take care of her. That's when Uncle Ray stepped in, and Auntie Carol not far behind. She lives in an apartment so couldn't offer us a place to stay. But maybe because of that, she's taken it on herself to be there for us in other ways.

So, she invented "family day," which we now have every Saturday.

It can be a lot, but today, it felt like a relief. Because it gave me something to think about, away from the bad dreams and the fire, and the elephant and Peter and all of New Warren. And most of all, it took my mind off sleepwalking, and my mom.

Because I know it isn't fair, but as I helped clean, all I could think about was my mom. I was kind of—no, *really*—mad at her.

Because see, she used to *know* when I sleepwalked.

I sleepwalked regularly until I was eight years old.

But even if I was up every night, I never woke up anywhere but my own room. Because my mom was always there to walk me back to bed.

Somehow she'd always know—sometimes she'd hear a noise, sometimes just get a feeling. We joked and called it her "mom superpower."

And it wasn't just that. She knew how to make me feel better about it too. The next morning, there was always a funny story. Apparently, when I was little at least, I was HILARIOUS when I sleepwalked. I would have conversations, answer questions, even describe my dreams.

There were so many mornings when I'd come into the kitchen to find my mom there, already doing her crossword and drinking her coffee.

"Mo!" she'd say. "You'll NEVER believe what you said last night, it was one for the ages."

"What did I say?" I'd ask eagerly.

"You were collecting balloons! According to you, they were everywhere. Striped ones, neon ones, sheep ones."

"Sheep ones?"

"Hey, you said it, not me. But why not? Sheep balloons in dreams? I love it . . ."

It was always funny. And no matter what, I knew my mom would be there to take care of me—to walk me back to my room, to keep me safe.

Now, here I was, for some reason doing it again, for the first time in years.

And what was I going to do: Add one more thing to my mom's plate by informing her that I was sleepwalking again? Tell her that among everything else she'd just lost, she'd also lost her mom superpowers?

No thank you.

Auntie Carol's car pulled into the driveway. I took a deep breath. Serenity squeaked like a rusty bike chain and ran to hide in his dog bed. Even he doesn't mess with Auntie Carol.

"My girls!" Auntie Carol said, leaning against the doorframe as she took off her shoes. "Come give your Auntie Carol a kiss!"

We sat down in the living room and Uncle Ray passed around carrot cake. I'm not 100 percent sure how he made it, but I think I saw avocado and squash go inside. I took a piece and nibbled the edges, to be polite.

"So how's New Warren treating you all?"

"So far so good," my mom said, after a beat of silence.

"Yes, congrats on the job!" Auntie Carol said. "Here's to a fresh start!" She raised her Starbucks cup. "Here's to a new chapter. Next stop, dating!"

I nearly spit out my water, and even CeCe looked up and frowned.

"What?! No!" my mom said. "I mean," she stumbled. "Right now I just need to get refocused. One thing at a time."

"Well," Auntie Carol said with a sigh. "Just remember, there are more fish in the sea. Also, you should call your mom. I give her all the updates, of course, but she wants to hear from you. Any nice young men at your new office?"

My mom clearly didn't know what to say, and Uncle Ray jumped in to rescue her.

"Well, uh, and the girls are having a great time at school. Right, CeCe?" he prompted.

"Yeah!" She grinned through a mouthful of carrot cake (she didn't mind the flecks of green inside, which shows you that five-year-olds are strange and unpredictable creatures).

"I'm going to Molly's house tomorrow!" And then

we heard more about the playdate, and CeCe's friends, and inevitably CeCe ran upstairs to get George to show him to Auntie Carol.

"And what about you, Miss Mo?" Auntie Carol asked, as CeCe tried to feed George carrot cake. "How's school?"

"Good," I said.

"Do you have any friends?"

"Some."

"Taking care of your mom and sister?"

"Of course," I said.

"I know you are, you always do." She patted me on the hand. "But really, you all need to get out more."

"We're fine, Auntie Carol, really," my mom said.

"Listen to her," Auntie Carol said, gesturing to *me*. "She's *not* okay. I thought it would be easier for Mo than for you and CeCe."

I whipped back, like I was stung. My mom and Auntie Carol didn't notice.

"But look," Auntie Carol went on, pointing at me. "She gives one word answers and barely smiles."

"She's twelve," my mom said. "She's fine."

"She's not fine," Auntie Carol said. "Look at her!"

"Um, she's right here!" I protested.

"How about you and CeCe go somewhere, Carol?" Uncle Ray said, cutting in again.

"Oh yes, you ALL need cheering up. What if I take you to mini golf?"

"Uh … fun," my mom said.

But there was no use fighting it—it was a done deal.

Because the mini golf place closest to New Warren is attached to Bryant's Farm, which serves homemade, delicious—

"THE MINI GOLF WITH THE ICE CREAM STAND?!" CeCe yelled, leaping to her feet. See? You try refusing that. Done deal.

"Perfect!" Auntie Carol said, clapping her hands. "Ray, you'll come too."

"Actuaaaally," he said, drawing out his words as he clearly thought of an excuse, "I have work. A big work project."

"And I agreed to help," I tacked on quickly. "So I can't go either."

He shot me a look, but didn't give me away.

"Too bad. So it's Lily and CeCe," Auntie Carol said, bouncing from disappointment to enthusiasm in the way only Auntie Carol can. "Let's get going!"

I watched them pile in and drive off. But once they were out of sight, I stayed at the window. Now I was looking at the junkyard. I could see the red of fire trucks past the fence, right by the giant, twisting oak tree at the edge of Uncle Ray's yard. From the window, it looked almost unreal, like a tree made of clay that had been twisted and bent unnaturally. If I climbed it, I bet I could see exactly what was happening in there . . .

"It's fine, Mo, really," Uncle Ray said from behind me. "There's nothing to worry about in the junkyard."

I nodded, though I wasn't convinced.

"You don't really have work, do you, Uncle Ray?" I asked.

"No," he admitted. "But you don't grow up with an older sister like Carol without learning to tell a few white lies. She means well, you know."

"I know," I said.

We were quiet for a minute.

"Do you want to talk about anything?" Uncle Ray asked.

"Want to listen to some music?" I asked.

"Sounds great," Uncle Ray said.

Uncle Ray didn't put in our CD. Instead, he took a few minutes to find the perfect record.

He didn't seem to want to talk either, which was perfect. As the music began, I sat back and let it wash over me.

Uncle Ray had said that music took him places.

I didn't understand what that meant at the time.

Until, as I listened, I stopped paying attention to the words and lyrics, and let the song lead me.

And I found myself in an unexpected place. A place I really didn't want to be.

CHAPTER 8

A MARBLE, A MEMORY

As "Goodnight Irene" by Mississippi John Hurt played, I found myself in a memory.

The last day I saw S-Dad—my stepdad—I was standing on the window seat in the kitchen, painting the wall. That's something you have to do to get a house ready to sell.

S-Dad was there to pick up his things.

He was leaving us—did I mention that?

We had no warning too. One night I heard raised voices, my mom crying, pleading, from downstairs.

The next morning, the house was quiet. I figured they'd had a fight but solved it. That happens. They'd been married for seven years, after all.

I was making toast for myself. But not just any. A special kind that S-Dad had taught me. It was cinnamon sugar toast, and you used the broiler on the toaster oven to get it to the perfect golden brown.

So I wasn't really paying attention when Mom and S-Dad came down with CeCe. If I had, I might have noticed how small and sad my mom looked.

When they said they wanted to talk with us, I was only half listening. The only thing I was thinking about was why were they bothering me while I was making delicious toast? And would they notice if I put more sugar on than I'm technically supposed to?

I had just put the toast in, and turned on the broiler, when he said it.

He didn't want to be married to Mom anymore. He'd be moving out. That day.

CeCe let out a sound just then, one I've never heard before. It was like a wail that's too awful to come out right. She ran from the room and my mom followed, calling her name.

"I know this is hard, Mo," S-Dad said, leaning against the kitchen countertop. "Be there for your mom and sister, okay? We'll still see each other, and—"

He went on, saying something. But all I could see, all I could hear, was "leaving . . . don't want to be . . . moving out today . . ."

With just a few words, our family was gone.

"I HATE YOU," I said. Now my voice was the one that sounded like the wail.

"Mo," he said, looking hurt. He took a step back.

I ran out the back door, into the yard, and up the steps to our tree house.

The one he and my mom had built for me.

I stayed there for a long time. And forgot about the toaster that I never turned off.

No one came to get me. I vowed I wouldn't go back inside.

Until the smoke, of course, and the fire alarm.

It was a small fire. No one got hurt.

But it cost a lot to fix the wall, especially since it had to be done so fast to sell the house.

And it felt like a sign. Like a punishment. Especially because when I went back inside, S-Dad was gone.

I've never been in a real fire. But that day, it felt like one had torn through our house.

Now, S-Dad talks with Mom about seeing CeCe for an afternoon, but not me. He says I made my feelings clear.

To a lot of people, this makes sense.

I'm only his stepdaughter, she's his real daughter.

I used to like math. It was clear-cut and reliable. But now, even math doesn't make sense. Because S-Dad is CeCe's dad, period. And she's only five. But he was my dad for *seven* years. Since *I* was five. He's the only dad I ever knew, the one who built me a tree house and went to all my plays, and took me to Six Flags when I won a history award in school.

And yet seven years somehow isn't enough.

Seven years isn't enough for him to send postcards and letters addressed to me. It's not enough for him to ask to see me on the weekends. It's not enough for Auntie Carol, and lots of other people, to think I should be sad. Our old neighbors, when it all happened, would flock to me, saying "At least you're okay!" or "It's not as hard for you!" or "You need to look after your mom and sister."

And I don't understand this terrible adult math that says that seven years is somehow not enough time to make a father.

Uncle Ray got up to let Serenity outside. The song had ended ages ago, and new songs had been playing, but I hadn't heard them.

Uncle Ray didn't say anything. Like he respected my quiet. But I'd had enough.

"I'm going for a walk," I said, standing abruptly.

"Okay," he said gently. "But only on sidewalks, and call me if you get lost or need a ride."

I nodded and practically tore out of the house.

Maybe Auntie Carol is right, I thought. *I need to get out more.*

Because being sad is AWFUL. Besides, my mom was doing enough of it for both of us. If I spent all my time being sad like my mom, who would look out for CeCe or my family?

I straightened my shoulders.

You're fine! I reminded myself.

I walked in circles around our block. Then, when I couldn't resist, I stopped and stood at the edge of the junkyard fence. I peered inside for a long, long time. It looked dark and foreboding. I swore the temperature was five degrees colder there, even though that's impossible—I was standing on Uncle Ray's street, with his house in sight.

Then, something caught my eye through the fence.

A whoosh of air escaped my throat.

I felt breathless, like I'd been running. No. It wasn't possible.

Because I could see it, almost reach it through the slats of the fence.

It was a blue marble. Luminous and bright.

Like the one I'd seen in my dream.

I foraged around the nearby bushes and trees until I found a long stick. I stuck it through the slats and gently rolled the marble out. It fell into my hand.

It was the marble from my dream. The one that had lit my way.

Except that now, on one side, it was charred black.

Like it had rolled through a fire and been covered in debris.

And then and there, I knew.

Uncle Ray was wrong. The junkyard WAS dangerous.

Because something was going on. Something BAD. Something to do with fire, and my dreams, and the marble I held in my hand.

I had to stop it, whatever it was.

It was up to me to take care of my family.

And I was afraid I knew exactly who to call.

CHAPTER 9

NEW WARREN,
PAST AND PRESENT

I thought the phone call would be weird. I mean, we were practically strangers, and I felt a tiny bit like a stalker looking him up in the school directory.

But when his mom handed him the phone, Nathaniel was SO EXCITED. He agreed to help immediately, even though I didn't really tell him what my problem was—I was worried that my mom or Uncle Ray would overhear. But even with my vagueness, he was happy to meet up. And he knew the perfect place.

That's how, at 10:00 A.M. on Sunday, I found myself at the New Warren Farmers' Market.

Apparently, the farmers' market is a big deal in New Warren, which just goes to show that this town really needs a movie theater. But it wasn't a long walk from Uncle Ray's, and Nathaniel lived right down the street from the center of town, so it was an ideal place to meet.

I spotted Nathaniel on the street corner.

"Mo!" he said as I approached. "Hi! How are you?

I'm glad you called, and—ghost!" He pointed up. "Did you see that?!" he asked. "Something moved. Ghost!"

I looked up to where he was pointing—a flagpole in front of town hall.

"Uh, I think that was the flag blowing in the breeze," I said.

As if on cue, the wind blew, and the flag fluttered.

"Oh. Well, maybe that's what I saw. Or maybe not!" he said brightly.

Hmmm, I thought. Suddenly, I wasn't so sure if Nathaniel was the ghost expert he said he was.

But before I could find an excuse to leave, he said, "Come on! Let's explore!"

And I couldn't think of a reason not to follow him.

"So," Nathaniel said, as we walked past food stalls, "I'm excited to help. But, uh, what is it you need help with, exactly? I don't think you said."

"Right," I said. I looked around. Everyone seemed busy. No one would overhear us.

"Well, uh, thank you for agreeing to meet." I could hear that I sounded weirdly formal, but how do you even talk about something like this? "I don't want to make a big thing of it, because I don't want anyone to find out. Especially my family. Okay?"

"Okay." He nodded, looking as serious as I think Nathaniel gets. "Keep it quiet. Got it."

"Great, thank you. So, um, I need to know more about the elephant story," I said finally. "And also the town legends about the, you know, hauntings."

"YOU SAW THE GHOST!!!" Nathaniel shouted.

"Shhh!" I said, as people looked our way. "We're keeping this quiet, remember?"

"Right," Nathaniel said, taking a deep breath and clearly trying to get ahold of himself.

"Where did you see it?" he asked.

"I don't really know if it was an actual ghost. Or if I believe in them. I mean, I respect your beliefs," I stumbled. "I just need information."

"But you saw something?"

"No, I had some strange dreams. And . . . some other small, weird things have been happening," I finished. I thought if I mentioned the marble Nathaniel might spontaneously combust with excitement. "I just need to know the facts. So I'm prepared."

"Prepared for when you face the ghost, got it," Nathaniel repeated in a slightly too-loud voice, nodding businesslike.

"Prepared on the very small, tiny, highly unlikely off chance that ghostly things are maybe possibly happening," I corrected, in what CeCe and I call our "inside voices."

"Right," Nathaniel said, getting the hint and matching my volume. "Okay. Cool. I'm cool. I'm happy to help. I'm calm."

I couldn't help but laugh.

"Thanks," I said. He *was* definitely trying. "I really appreciate it."

"I know where to start looking," Nathaniel said. "You know the whole tourist campaign? Town hall has an exhibit up now—I saw it the last time I was there. It's small, but it definitely has some good stuff."

"Great," I said.

Town hall was an old light blue building with a pointed tower at the top that I'm sure has a cool official name.

The exhibit was right inside, along with "Discover New Warren" pamphlets and brochures from local restaurants and B and Bs.

Nathaniel was right—it was small. It was just a wall filled with a sleek timeline, which showed important moments from New Warren's history. There were photos of the town when it was mostly just fields, and a big thing about how New Warren contributed to the Revolutionary War.

Then, there was the circus, and the ghost story.

The display read:

In 1901, local resident Thomas P. Childers brought Flying Brothers Circus to New Warren on the first leg of his inaugural East Coast Tour. Disaster struck when a fire broke out on opening night. The fire, either caused by a lightning strike or an overturned lantern (sources differ on the cause), inflicted significant damage. Over fifty people were injured in the subsequent rush to exit the tent. Miraculously, the only fatality was a nonhuman one. Maudie, a female Asian elephant, one of the circus's star attractions, died in the flames. While many details of the fire have since been lost, the legacy of the fire, and Maudie the elephant, remain. Residents have reported supernatural sightings in the area ever since. In 1954, nine-year-old Jimmy Gilbert reported that he was saved from drowning by a ghostly elephant who lifted him to safety (though police reports suggest it was a tree branch). It's rumored that if you look out your window on a clear and quiet night, you might see her parading the streets of New Warren, keeping its residents safe.

Next to the write-up were two pictures.

One was a formal portrait of a man in a top hat. It was labeled:

Thomas P. Childers, founder, Flying Brothers Circus.

He had a stern face and didn't look very friendly. But then again, that might have been the old photography.

The other was kind of grainy. But there she was—
Maudie the elephant. In the photo, she was standing
in a field, with the circus tent going up behind her.
Thomas Childers, still in his top hat, stood next to her.
It was labeled:

Thomas P. Childers and Maudie the elephant
preparing for their New Warren performance.

And that was it.

It was kind of weird. Maudie the elephant was being
used for all the "Discover New Warren" ads, but this
exhibit only had one photo of her, and a kind of faraway one at that. I got closer and peered at the image. I
wished I could see more. I wished I could see her face,
not just her blurry outline.

"Is that who you saw?" Nathaniel whispered, awed.

"I don't know," I said. "I mean, I saw an elephant. And
she's an elephant. But I don't recognize anything specific."

I scanned the rest of the image, trying to look at
everything more closely.

Thomas Childers was still wearing his big top hat,
and still didn't look like someone I'd want to be friends
with.

They were standing in a big field, in a time when
New Warren clearly had fewer buildings. The field

was mostly grass, and you could see where there were big poles already set up behind them for the circus tent.

Otherwise it seemed ordinary. The sky was clear. There were a few trees at the edges, young ones. One was a little stranger than the others.

It was small but already twisting, as though its trunk had been wrung like a cloth. And there was a funny little nook forming, like something had scooped out a chunk of it, and the branches were tilting toward where the tent stood, like it wanted to peer inside . . .

I froze.

I looked again.

"What is it?" Nathaniel asked, noticing my expression.

"The tree," I managed to say.

"Huh?"

"The tree." I pointed. "That's the tree in Uncle Ray's yard. I'm sure of it."

We looked at each other, our eyes wide.

It had all happened right next door.

CHAPTER 10

GHOSTS ARE
(PROBABLY) NOT REAL

"This doesn't mean I believe in ghosts," I said, for what felt like the fifteenth time. "It's probably just a coincidence."

"The fire? Happening on a night you dreamed about fire, in the place where the fire literally happened? What are the chances?" Nathaniel asked, also for the fifteenth time.

We were sitting on the curb by town hall, looking out on the farmers' market. We'd been having this discussion for a while.

"Just do me a favor," Nathaniel said. "Keep an open mind. Maybe it isn't a ghost. But maybe . . ." He looked at me hopefully.

"I'll keep an open mind," I said. "Though I still think it's probably all just a big coincidence."

Nathaniel nodded happily. There was quiet for a moment, and I watched some tourists being talked at enthusiastically by a white, gray-haired man with a visor and a clipboard. It looked like he was trying to sell them something.

"So, what next?" I asked. "You being the ghost expert and all. If there is a ghost—and I'm just saying *if*— what do we do? How do we find out more?"

"Hm . . . ," Nathaniel said. "I think we have to go to the library. The public library is almost as old as New Warren; there has to be something there. We can go tomorrow after school."

I nodded. It was a solid plan—or at least, better than any plan I could come up with at the moment. Besides, when in doubt, the library always seems like a nice idea.

I was looking at Nathaniel, so I didn't notice the man with the clipboard until he was right in front of us.

"Hello!" he said. "Welcome to New Warren! Would you like some fun facts about our historical architecture?"

"Uh, no we're fine. Thank you," I said.

"Where are you two visiting from?" the man asked, undeterred.

"I live here," Nathaniel said.

"Ah wonderful," the man said. He looked at me expectantly.

"Me too," I said.

The man was wearing big round glasses that made him look kind of like an owl. So you could *really* tell how surprised he was by my answer. I thought his eyes were going to pop out of his head, like a cartoon.

"You're from *here*? New Warren?" he asked, like I'd declared I had wings.

I wanted to say: "Well, technically I just moved here, but also why is this so hard to believe?"

But instead I said, "Yes. I live here. In New Warren."

The man stared with googly eyes, and Nathaniel frowned, confused.

Then, a familiar voice saved us.

"There you are!" Uncle Ray said, waving from across the grass, a bag bulging with greens swinging at his side. "Want a ride home?"

"We have to go," I said.

"Oh, all right," the man said. "Well, happy touring, I mean, uh . . ."

He trailed off and went to accost someone else, and Uncle Ray came walking across the green toward us.

"I've never seen Unofficial Tour Guide act so strangely," Nathaniel said as we got to our feet.

"Unofficial Tour Guide?" I asked.

"Yeah, he just wanders around New Warren trying to tell people about historical sites," Nathaniel said. "He doesn't get paid or anything."

New Warren, as I think I've mentioned before, was turning out to be a VERY strange place.

"I don't know why he was being so weird, though," Nathaniel said. I opened my mouth but didn't have time to explain.

"Who's this?!" Uncle Ray asked, grinning as he reached us.

"This is Nathaniel," I said. "We're doing a, uh, project for school." I waited for a beat, wondering what Nathaniel would say.

See, Uncle Ray stood out. First, he was pretty much the only Asian face I'd seen in the crowd (and almost the only non-white face I'd seen too). Then there was his hair, and his glasses, and his Grateful Dead T-shirt. When he walked by, people stared; I'd seen it.

But Nathaniel didn't stare, or laugh, or act like anything else but his normal self. He smiled and reached out his hand to shake Uncle Ray's, like an adult.

"Nice to meet you," he said.

Uncle Ray shook his hand so excitedly it was like a dance move.

"Nice to meet you! Great to meet a friend of Mo's! You should come over for dinner sometime! Look at these vegetables!"

And then he talked about something called kohlrabi all the way back to the car.

As Uncle Ray loaded the trunk, I walked with

Nathaniel to the crosswalk. He lived down the street, in one of the big houses just off the center of town.

"Thanks," I said. It felt like I was saying thank you for a lot of things. For his help today, for not laughing at Uncle Ray, for even answering the phone and agreeing to help after I'd been not the nicest to him in the school library.

"No problem," he said. "We'll figure this out. Even"—he gave a dramatic sigh, like this was the most inconceivable thing in the world—"if it *isn't* a ghost."

"Which it proooobably isn't," I added, smiling in spite of myself.

He grinned, but then looked serious.

"But for real, Mo. I'll help you," he said earnestly. "Whatever it is. You don't have to do this alone."

"Thanks," I said again. I hoped he knew how much that "thanks" held.

On an impulse, I held out my fist to him, and we fist-bumped.

Uncle Ray and I drove home, and New Warren town center—the old part of town—fled past the window. I wondered what it had been like when Maudie the elephant was here. I wondered if she'd walked on these same streets, if she'd stood by town hall, or performed for a crowd on the town green.

I took a deep breath to steady myself.

Tomorrow, we'd go to the library. We'd figure this out.

And what a nice idea—that whatever happened, whatever was going on at Uncle Ray's house, I didn't have to face it alone.

CHAPTER 11

MONDAY MONDAY

Before we could get to the library, though, I had to face the school day.

I'd forgotten all about Ms. Shay (though in fairness to me, I did have a lot going on).

But Ms. Shay hadn't forgotten about me.

In fact, she was waiting outside math, my last class before lunch.

I mouthed "Sorry" to Nathaniel, who'd been waiting for me. As she marched me to the guidance office, he made a sympathetic face, then retreated to the library.

Ms. Shay's office was a small rectangle off the main hallway. It was one of the only rooms with a door, and even though it had a window leading to the hall, there were posters covering it, which I liked. I was glad every passing person couldn't see me in there.

Ms. Shay, like her office, was cheerful but no-nonsense. I'm sure she was a great person for other kids to talk to. But I didn't need to talk. And our conversation went something like this:

Ms. Shay: So, Mo, how are you doing?

Me: I'm fine.

Ms. Shay: And how's New Warren treating you?

Me: It's fine.

Ms. Shay: Tell me about your new house.

Me: Also fine.

I mean really. How many different ways can adults find to ask me if I'm okay?

And the answer is also: "Yes I'm fine, leave me alone."

Besides, what was I supposed to say?

Especially when Ms. Shay asked, "Is there anything you want to ask me about?" I wasn't really thinking and actually answered truthfully.

"Yeah, have you ever heard about the elephant ghost?"

"Mo, changing the subject won't work with me," Ms. Shay said, gently but firmly.

I fought down what I was thinking, which was *ARGH*. And also: *Don't ask a question if you don't want the answer!*

Just as the bell was about to ring, when I thought it couldn't get any worse, Ms. Shay said, "Let's meet up again soon, Mo."

My feelings must have shown on my face.

"I'm not all that bad, am I?" Ms. Shay said with a smile. "I think it would be good, help us get to know each other, help you adjust. And maybe one of these days we can have your mom in too."

It was like there was ice under my skin.

"Uh, she's busy," I said. "You really shouldn't bother her. Meeting up again sounds great!"

Ms. Shay looked at me suspiciously, but also smiled and nodded. I fled as soon as I could.

That was *just* what I didn't need. My mom had enough to worry about without adding me and the middle school guidance counselor to the list.

After school, I couldn't wait to get to the bus.

We were taking Nathaniel's, which would drop us off in the center of town, just a block away from the public library.

From the bus window, I could see Peter in the car pickup area, holding a duffel bag with a baseball bat inside it. He got into a red car, driven by a man who could only be his dad, with the same straw-colored hair.

I felt a jolt in my chest when I heard a sound from the car—a raised voice, like his dad was yelling. Ever since the summer, angry sounds have had that effect on me.

But this wasn't S-Dad, I reminded myself, willing my heart back to its normal rhythm. This wasn't that kind of yelling. This was Peter, and he'd probably done something that his dad was legitimately mad about.

I took a deep breath and listened hard to something Nathaniel was saying about the library, and turned my thoughts away from Peter.

The bus ride was nice, though I had to remind Nathaniel to keep his voice down about every three minutes, to keep the entire bus from knowing what we were up to.

The New Warren Public Library is a big, friendly brick building. It made me finally understand the word "stately." It was like a relative who's fun to hang out with, but also really wants you to take your elbows off the table.

I followed Nathaniel to the archive room, and a librarian pointed us toward the shelf where we'd find all the books on town history. And then, there was nothing to do but dive in.

Research sounds like it could be fun. I mean you're discovering things, right? We were in this giant, fancy room, surrounded by researchers either reading, typing, or talking in hushed voices. It was the perfect setting.

I could imagine a movie scene here, with a research montage. There'd be books and pages flipping, and after a few minutes someone would yell "AHA!" And then you'd be done and you'd know the answer. You'd think it would all be really exciting.

But apparently not. In fact, at first, research was really, really boring.

Because a LOT of people have written books about New Warren, which surprised me. Some were general histories, one was about authors who've lived here, another was a collection of old town documents. And we had to look through them *all*.

I found "Childers, tax records" and "Childers, family ownings" which was just a bunch of hard-to-read, tiny maps.

Nathaniel found a mention of some Childers from the 1700s who fought in the Revolutionary War. But after two long hours, it was looking like we might never find it. Until suddenly . . .

"Mo!" Nathaniel gasped.

"Shhh," a researcher said from across the table.

Nathaniel winced and continued on in a whisper.

"I found something," he said. He scooched his chair next to me and laid it out. It was a paperback book, and as Nathaniel brought it closer, I could see a big picture of the author on the back. He was a young white man with brown hair and round wide eyes. He looked familiar somehow. But then Nathaniel was shoving the pages under my nose, and it fell out of my head.

"Here!" Nathaniel said. He put his finger to the passage, and read:

"Thomas Childers was a true son of New Warren. His great-grandfather was among the town's founders, though by the time Thomas was born, the family wealth had been greatly reduced.

"An enterprising young man, Childers turned to the circus—that beacon of social mobility that catapulted many a dreamer to fame and fortune in the late 1800s. As many circus pioneers did, he began with human displays, collecting an array of spectacles including conjoined twins and a 'giant' (probably a man with what today would be diagnosed as a hormone imbalance leading to increased growth). While his human 'zoo' ultimately dispersed after performers complained of underpayment and harsh conditions, Childers was still financially successful enough to make his name in the circus industry.

"Childers used his growing success to entice investors and finally construct his own traveling circus, the crown jewel of which was the purchase of an elephant, who Childers named Maudie. We can only imagine how Childers felt on his return to New Warren at the start of the first official tour of Thomas Childers's Flying Brothers Circus. As he paraded into town, to joyful music, with a towering elephant behind him that would leave townsfolk awestruck, he must have felt triumphant.

"That his triumph turned so quickly into ashes may explain Childers's later breakdown. The very next day, a fire devastated the circus.

"When it comes to the events of the fire, accounts vary. In records and letters, Childers claims a bolt of lightning from an unexpected spring storm hit the tent, causing a fire that no reasonable man could anticipate or control. However, some eyewitness accounts, records in letters and reports to town officials, claim that the fire began after an altercation involving Childers himself. According to witnesses, Maudie the elephant froze on stage, prompting Childers to hit her with a bullhook—a metal curved hook used as a tool of animal management, and which was considered an effective and acceptable tool for animal training at the time. According to these accounts, the blow caught a low-hanging lantern, knocking it aside and sparking a fire. Whatever happened, in the ensuing panic, the damage was extensive.

Not only was the entire tent burned beyond repair, but Maudie the elephant—Childers's central investment—was killed in the ensuing flames."

Nathaniel stopped suddenly.

"Are you okay, Mo?"

I had hidden my face in my hands without meaning to.

"Yes," I squeaked, hoping Nathaniel couldn't see that my eyes were squeezed shut behind my palms. "Go on. Get it over with."

"Uh, okay . . ." I didn't need to see him to know he wasn't sure what to do and was considering stopping. But after a beat, he kept reading.

"We will never know what happened that evening, and what truly caused the disastrous fire. But whatever its cause, its effects were devastating. Any money made from the tour was lost as investors pulled out, and as New Warren charged Childers with significant fines for damage caused by the fire, and for the elephant's burial.

"Childers retired to New Warren a broken man. Tormented by his failure, this once clear-eyed dreamer became convinced that he was haunted by the ghost of Maudie the elephant. By the end of his life, Childers was identifying ghosts in everything, most notably a large white dog, who he claimed was Maudie come back to take her revenge. In life, Maudie had loved dogs and had one as a companion until her death. This undoubtedly caused Childers's strange belief that his former elephant followed him, and it was these ramblings of an unhinged man that gave rise to the rumors of animal ghosts that have persisted in New Warren to this day."

Nathaniel stopped and looked at me nervously, like I was going to faint or break into a million pieces.

"I'm *fine*," I insisted. I realized I would sound more convincing if I took my hands away from my face. "I just . . . that was just a lot."

"Yeah," Nathaniel said. "I don't know about this guy."

"It seems like the writer wants us to like him," I said, finally peeling my hands away. "But I don't know . . ."

I leaned back in my chair. The stuff about the

fire had bothered me. I mean, *of course* it had. But also . . .

"Yeah, something about this that feels off," Nathaniel said.

"Excellent," a new voice cut in. "That's because you're reading between the lines."

We started and looked up. A tall woman with dark skin, purple lipstick, glittery cat-eye glasses, and a name tag that said, "Lavender P, Jr. Librarian," smiled down at us.

"You have to read between the lines when you're a researcher," she said. "Some people want history to be all one way, and they'll ignore the hard or bad parts to fit their vision. Here."

She picked up the book and scanned the passage.

"Okay, so," she began to list, counting off with her fingers.

"One: Childers exploited lots of people and the author basically says 'That's okay.'

"Two: Whenever anyone says something was okay because it was a 'common practice,' do some digging. I'm sure there were people who thought animal abuse wasn't great in Childers's time too.

"And three: The author wants us to think that the cause of the fire is this big mystery, but it isn't—it sounds like lots of people saw Childers beat Maudie and cause the fire, which is awful. But the author doesn't want to think about that, because then the elephant is the victim, not Childers."

She put the book down between us, careful to keep it open to the right page.

"See?" she said. "This author is biased. You both did a great job in identifying that. You're natural historians."

"Whoa," I said.

"That was like a magic trick!" Nathaniel said.

I nodded in agreement. She'd brought all the things that had been bugging me, but that I couldn't quite put into words, out onto the surface.

"I'm Lavender," she said with a smile, offering her hand to shake. "I'm the new research librarian."

Nathaniel introduced himself, and when she turned to him, I noticed that Lavender's hair was dyed purple on one side. She was, undoubtedly, the coolest person I had met in all of New Warren.

"I'm Mo," I said, shaking her hand. "I'm new too. I mean, I just moved here."

"Nice," she said with a smile. "We should compare notes sometime."

I grinned—I would like that.

"Well"—Lavender glanced at her watch—"sorry to interrupt you. I just can't resist an opportunity to analyze a text. And to meet young researchers, of course. If you ever need research help, let me know. There's a lot of dirt here in New Warren, and I'm making it my personal mission to uncover it."

She gave us one more beaming smile, and then she was off, striding toward the archive desk.

"Wow," I sighed, watching her go. "She is SO COOL."

"Yeah," Nathaniel said. "I'd pay to watch her debate this author."

"Right?!" I giggled. And then stopped when someone hushed us sternly.

Apparently, archives are not for giggling.

But it had been great to meet Lavender. And it had taken my mind off Thomas Childers. And the fire.

We didn't think we'd find much more, but Nathaniel realized there were pictures at the back of the book. He took a second to flip through.

"Yeah, there's nothing much here," Nathaniel said (quietly) while I put the rest of our books in a stack to return. "It's mostly fields, oh a cow in a field! And the church when it was just being built, and a very exciting picture of another field, and—"

Nathaniel got quiet so fast it was like sound screeched to a halt.

"Nathaniel?" I asked, still stacking.

"Um, what did you say you saw in your dream?" Something about his voice made me look up at him.

His eyes were big. "Marbles, right? And the elephant had . . ."

"You mean the bell?" I asked. "Yeah, it was just a weird dream detail."

"Right," he said. "But also you haven't read any books about New Warren, right? Or seen any photos of the time period, or circuses of the time, or anything?"

"No, why would I?" I asked. "What's go—"

"Here." Nathaniel passed the book to me, open at one of the picture pages. "It's a poster for the circus."

"Okay," I said, wondering if now Nathaniel was the one who needed to lie down. I peered at the image.

It was a scan of an old, yellowed poster. It had clearly been used to advertise that the circus was coming to town.

It read:

MAUDIE THE DANCING ELEPHANT

AT THOMAS CHILDERS'S FLYING BROTHERS CIRCUS

ONE LUCKY CHILD WILL WIN A GIFT FROM MAUDIE HERSELF!

And then there was an illustration of an elephant. An elephant who looked very familiar. An elephant who wore a thick, red woven cord around her neck.

She was holding out her trunk to the viewer. And in her trunk, she held a blue marble.

And below it all, hanging from the red cord, hung a tiny, delicate silver bell.

CHAPTER 12

DANGER ZONE

When you suddenly find out that ghosts are real, your definition of danger has to budge. Even if just a little bit.

That's why I was willing to do something that felt more dangerous than anything I'd ever done before. It was clear we had to find out what was going on. We had to get to the source.

And the source—where it all began, where the fire broke out, and where Maudie the elephant was buried, and now haunted—was right next door.

So we were going to break in to the old town junkyard.

The date was easy (and terrifying) to pick—Halloween.

"Halloween is the PERFECT night," Nathaniel said. "A lot of ghost researchers think that Halloween is when ghosts are at their most active. We're sure to see her then."

I won't lie—the idea of going on Halloween made our plan feel extra scary. But I couldn't argue with Nathaniel's logic. Besides, Halloween was that weekend, and it was the perfect time to sneak away. CeCe would be out trick-or-treating, Nathaniel and I could tell our parents we were out with friends, and with all the noise and hubbub of the night, we could get into the junkyard, and then get back out again, with no one knowing.

Or at least, that was the plan.

The next day, Nathaniel and I sat down at lunch to figure out just how we'd do it.

"Mo! Ghost update!" Nathaniel said loudly as I walked toward our table.

"Shhhh!" I said, glancing at the book stacks. "Keep your voice down. We don't know who else is here."

"Right," Nathaniel whispered. "I was just excited. Look! I found a map of the junkyard," he went on in a normal voice now, but at least not a yell. He slid his laptop around to show me the screen. "The back stretches against an old rock quarry, so I don't think we want to go in that way. I think the best place to get in might be your yard. We can get over the fence behind the house."

"Great plan," I said. "I'll scout it out today when I get home."

"Excellent," Nathaniel said. He looked at his sandwich like he was contemplating it, then put it down and went for his chips instead.

I opened my lunch and examined my own sandwich.

It was . . . lettuce? With . . . hummus? And some sort of . . . pink vegetable? I sniffed it suspiciously.

"That looks AMAZING," Nathaniel said.

"For real?" I asked. "It's like a plant store in bread."

"Well, mine's pastrami and rye," he said with a disapproving wrinkle of his nose. "It's my dad's favorite, and when he makes lunch, he just makes us all the same thing to save time."

"Uh, that sounds INCREDIBLE," I said.

Nathaniel paused, then looked at me hopefully. I looked at him hopefully.

Without saying a word, we switched sandwiches, and I can tell you for a fact that I got the better deal.

"Oh, by the way," Nathaniel said after a happy bite. "Welcome!"

"Huh?"

"To Library Lunch Club! Population one, now two!"

I smiled.

"It's an honor," I said.

We cheersed with our sandwiches, then dug in.

As we ate, I wondered if, after all of this, we'd still hang out. We were very different people, after all, and the only reason we were spending time together was Maudie. Besides, I'd told myself that I didn't need friends in New Warren, right?

All this made my stomach feel like there were rocks in there, instead of delicious pastrami. So I pushed the thoughts away for another time.

We'd finished eating, and were going over our plans one more time, when I heard footsteps coming toward us. And then, the sound of a familiar, less-than-welcome voice.

"Whatcha doing?" Peter asked, peering from one of the bookshelves. "Is this the part of the movie where the losers team up?"

"Go away, Peter," I said. I snapped Nathaniel's laptop shut.

"I'm just being friendly," Peter said.

I shook my head and began putting my things in my bag.

Nathaniel sat there, silently, looking at his hands, his cheeks red. He wasn't making a move, so I grabbed his lunch things.

"Come on, Nathaniel," I said. "Let's go."

"Wow, I was just saying *hi*," Peter said, like WE were the ones being unreasonable.

I breezed by him, and after a moment, Nathaniel followed.

"I do NOT like that guy," I said, once we were safely in the hallway.

"Well," Nathaniel sighed quietly. "He's complicated. And I don't think he means the things he says. He thinks he's funny. Like a class clown."

"Well, he can be a class clown with someone else," I said, feeling like I'd just swallowed a very sour candy. "As long as he stays away from me."

"Fair," Nathaniel said. And for a moment he sounded a little . . . sad? But then the bell rang, and we raced to class, and I didn't have a chance to ask him about it.

Uncle Ray was on the phone when I got home, which I knew he would be. Uncle Ray, it's turning out, is a very social butterfly. On Tuesdays he talks to Phil, a friend from his touring days, who worked in lighting and lives in LA. On Thursdays he has a group Zoom with some friends in New York. And every other Friday, he goes to meet up with friends in Boston. And that's not mentioning all the phone catchups and group texts he fits in with other friends from his music days.

I waved as I came in and yelled "Hi, Phil!" and then went upstairs to work.

I was on my bed, finishing my math homework, when the front door slammed. I heard pounding feet, and CeCe burst into the room. She threw herself on her bed, her backpack still on, and buried her head in her pillow.

"CeCe?" I asked, jumping up. "What's wrong?"

She looked up at me, her face red and tracked with tears.

"What is it?" I asked, sitting on the bed and putting a hand on her shoulder.

"I'm sad," she said, almost angrily. "That's what's wrong."

"Did something happen at school?" I asked.

"NO," she said, this time definitely angrily. "I'm just sad. I can be sad."

"Oh, okay," I said. "Well, let's go play a game and cheer you up."

"I don't want to play! I want to be sad!" she yelled, bunching her hands up in little fists. "Aren't you sad sometimes?"

"No," I said, sharper than I'd meant to. "I'm not. I'm too busy to be sad. Now come on, let's go watch a movie. Wouldn't that be a special treat? A movie will help you feel better . . ."

It took more coaxing, but I finally ushered her downstairs and sat her in front of one of her favorite cartoons, with a snack in hand. Her tears dried, and though she looked at me with big eyes every once in a while, she didn't say anything after that. By the time my mom got home from work, everything felt like normal.

Phew, I thought. *One less worry.*

After dinner, Uncle Ray asked me if I felt like a song.

For all his quirkiness, Uncle Ray seemed to be the *only* adult around me who realized that all the "Are you okay do you want to talk?" stuff was NOT what I needed.

So now, when he sat down, he'd just look over and ask: "Good?"

"Good," I'd reply.

And then he'd lean forward, and press play.

I wanted to listen to the lyrics, or just plain zone out. But I had so much on my mind that night: CeCe, and Peter, and the junkyard, and Maudie, and everything Nathaniel and I were trying to do. So as "Under Pressure" by Queen began to play, and its beats came fast and nonstop, my mind began to race along with it. My brain, as if responding to my worries, reached back in time to find some more.

And I found myself in a memory.

It never bothered me that I didn't know my dad. My mom says they were really young, and he wasn't ready to be a dad. I've never met him, so I can't miss him. And up until I was five, it was just me and my mom. The perfect family.

So I wasn't happy when my mom began dating S-Dad, who then was just "Jim." I didn't understand why he needed to be around all the time. I didn't want to share my mom. And I didn't want him to hurt her.

I remember the day that Jim won me over. He and my mom took me apple picking. He picked apples from the tallest branches, and then he caught my eye, and began to juggle the apples in his hand.

"WOW!" I gasped.

"Cool, right?" he said with a grin. "I was the class clown—I used to do this all the time in school. I can teach you, if you want."

And suddenly, just like that, I liked Jim. I told my mom that I didn't mind if he spent time with us.

In fact, all of a sudden, I liked the idea.

Soon, we had a new kind of family. One with two adults, and a mom who was happy and smiling, and who didn't have to work so hard. Now she had someone to drive when she was tired, or to bring her coffee in the morning.

It made me happy.

Then all of a sudden, there was CeCe.

This new person I was related to.

She's my half sister technically, but from the moment I saw her, I knew we were the same. We were *all* family.

But S-Dad forgot that.

He has a new family now. That's the worst part. That's the part I think that tipped my mom from sad to something else. He has a new wife, new baby, new house, and here we are with all the messy leftover pieces.

I've been thinking back to that day in the apple orchard a lot these past few months.

I wish I could go back and tell my younger self that he was bad: that you should never let your guard down, and never trust a class clown. I wish I could tell my younger self that danger is *everywhere*.

If I'd known then, maybe I could have kept my family safe.

But, of course, I can't do that.

So instead, I'll do what S-Dad won't. *I'll* be here for my family. Nothing else will happen to us, not on my watch.

I won't let anything that dangerous come near us ever again.

"Whatcha think?" Uncle Ray asked.

The music was over.

"I think I have a lot to do," I said.

I said good night maybe a little more abruptly than I meant to, and did my nightly check.

My mom put CeCe to bed that night, which was new (though she forgot to tuck in George and sing him a song, which CeCe insists on. I took care of it later, after my mom had gone).

I lay in my own bed and listened to CeCe's even breathing, and tried to let all the worries and feeling drain from my brain. *Everything is okay*, I told myself. *Everything will be okay. You'll find a way to keep them all safe.* I repeated it like a magic charm, again and again, and for a moment, it seemed to work. Because I fell asleep, which means that for a little while, I let my worries go.

Which was why it was all the more jarring when I opened my eyes . . .

. . . and circus music began to play.

CHAPTER 13

A SHORT . . . DREAM?

I was in Uncle Ray's front yard.

In the distance, over the junkyard fence, I could hear music. It was circus music, meant to be bright and cheery and welcoming. But somehow it was also brittle and tinny, like the strained, worn-down sound on Uncle Ray's oldest records.

I heard a cheer, and excited faraway voices. And then, there she was.

Maudie the elephant, silver and white and translucent, stood by the fence at the edge of Uncle Ray's yard. I tried to step toward her, but it was like my feet were rooted into the ground. Like something wanted to keep us apart.

"I know what happened!" I yelled into the night, not caring if I was awake or asleep. "It wasn't your fault!"

She looked at me with sad eyes, and then her trunk moved, reaching out to me. The wind blew, the eerie music caught up in its howl.

"It wasn't your fault!" I said again. "He shouldn't have treated you that way!"

And for a moment, I think I woke up.

All of a sudden, I felt my bare feet against the cold wet of the grass.

It was dark outside, and freezing.

And there wasn't an elephant standing in front of me, but a dog, right where she had stood. A big, ghostly white dog, who seemed to glow in the muted light of the moon.

"Maudie?" I whispered. "It's you, isn't it?"

Then, everything went black.

I woke up in the living room, with early morning light practically poking at my eyelids through the downstairs window. I was on the couch, part of me stretched out, the other half sitting up. My back was a giant OW.

One of my bedroom blankets was half on me, like it had fallen on just one of my legs while I was sleeping. I must have grabbed it and taken it with me while I was sleepwalking.

"That was so weird," I said out loud. And yes, I was talking to myself, but the dream had been even weirder than that. *It was just a dream*, I reminded myself. *A sleepwalking dream. It wasn't real . . .*

I began to get up, and then caught sight of my feet. They were dirty, despite my shower last night, and covered in clumps of something.

I looked closer.

My feet were covered in wet grass.

But also dirt. And . . . I smelled my foot, as gross as it sounds.

It was soot.

Like something had been buried but wasn't staying that way.

Like a fire had been set, or was burning, somewhere I couldn't see.

And it was getting closer.

CHAPTER 14

HALLOWEEN HIJINKS

The night of Halloween came so fast, it felt like the calendar had sped up, just for us.

I helped CeCe put the finishing touches on her mermaid-oceanographer costume (George featured heavily, of course). My mom was taking her trick-or-treating and had even pinned a few paper seashells to an old sweater, to go along with CeCe's theme.

"Are you sure you don't want me to take her?" I asked, just before Nathaniel was set to arrive for dinner. "She'll be really upset if you're not out for at least an hour."

"Yes, I'm sure, Mo," my mom had said with a huff. "Go have fun with your friend. I'm *fine*," she said, in response to a skeptical look I hadn't meant to give her but did all the same.

I felt a cluster of feelings in my stomach: worry that my mom would flake and disappoint CeCe, relief that our plans were still on, and a healthy dollop of TER-ROR for the junkyard and everything that lay ahead. On top of it all was the wish that I could tell my mom everything like I used to in Ridgemont, and that she would help, and know what to do.

I took a deep breath, swallowed my feelings, and nodded.

Nathaniel had already met Uncle Ray, but now he got to meet my mom and CeCe. My mom was mostly quiet, but CeCe made up for that. Nathaniel did a great job listening to her talk about the ins and outs of life as a mermaid who was also an award-winning scientist. The only one who didn't seem to like Nathaniel was Serenity, and since Serenity hates everyone except Uncle Ray, I told him not to take it personally.

We sat down to an early dinner of chickpea loaf. It's not my favorite, but Saturdays are chickpea loaf night for Uncle Ray. He offered to make something else, but it didn't seem fair to make him rearrange his life any more than he has.

Besides, focusing on pretending to enjoy chickpea loaf was a good distraction from thinking about ghosts, the junkyard, and our possible impending doom.

We all talked about our Halloween plans. Uncle Ray was leaving for a friend's Halloween party, my mom and CeCe would head out trick-or-treating, and Nathaniel and I told everyone that we'd be meeting up with friends down the road to watch a scary movie.

Overall, things went well, and uneventfully.

Until Uncle Ray said: "So what's the project you two are working on?"

"Huh?" I asked before I could stop myself.

"I thought you two were working on a school project," he said. "Isn't that what you were doing at town hall and the library?"

"Right," Nathaniel said. "The project. It's for school, about—" He faltered, sounding very obviously like he was trying to make something up.

"About a dog!" I cut in.

"That's right!" Nathaniel said. I'd filled him in about my most recent dreams.

"I saw a stray around here," I went on. "We want to rescue it, and our social studies teacher said we could do a project on strays and shelters."

"Yes," Nathaniel echoed. "Definitely that. Is what we're doing."

"Oh, is it that big white dog?" Uncle Ray asked.

We both bolted upright.

"You know it?" Nathaniel asked, his eyes big, his excitement barely kept in his skin.

"Oh yeah. I see it around the neighborhood all the time. But wait—" Uncle Ray cocked his head and frowned. "You know, it's funny—you're right. I don't know who it belongs to. I just assumed it was Mrs. Smith's dog, or some other neighbor. But I've seen it around ever since I moved in. Come to think of it, that dog must be *ancient*. I moved in more than fifteen years ago . . ." He frowned again, then shrugged his shoulders as if to say, *Oh well, it's a mystery*. "Well, that's a great project. Let me know if I can help."

Nathaniel and I looked at each other, eyes wide.

Uncle Ray had been seeing the ghost ever since he moved in. He just didn't know it.

After dinner, we helped to clean up, and then it was time. My mom and CeCe left first, followed quickly by Uncle Ray.

Nathaniel and I got out our supplies—flashlights, Nathaniel's camera to document what we found, and . . .

"You brought a saltshaker?" I asked.

"I read somewhere that you can use it to keep evil out. If we run into anything bad, we'll make a salt circle around ourselves and we should be fine," Nathaniel said.

"*Should* be fine?" I asked.

"Well, it's usually for things like demons, not ghosts. But I'm sure it will work!" he said brightly.

I felt a little less reassured. But the brightness of the flashlights (which were camping flashlights, and VERY powerful) made me feel better.

I led Nathaniel to the tree, just outside my bedroom window, with the low overhanging branches—the one I'd recognized from the photo.

Since it was my idea, it seemed only fair that I go first.

I climbed onto the lowest branches of the tree, and then sidled out, toward the fence. It had slats running through it, so from the height of the branch, it was easy to get my hands and feet into the sides of the fence. I swung my leg over the top, and imagined that this was how mountain climbers must feel.

I edged down the other side of the fence, careful to only move one foot at a time, one arm at a time. The wood on the inside of the fence wasn't painted and was splintering. I moved extra cautiously, and only got poked a few times. Finally, I was close enough to the ground that with a light hop, I was on the junkyard floor.

"Okay, I'm here. Your turn," I called softly over the fence. "Oh, also, be careful of splinters!"

There was the sound of scraping and tree rustling, which meant Nathaniel was making his way over.

While I waited, I turned on my flashlight and looked around.

The junkyard was a maze of heaps of, well, *junk*. In the beam of my light, I saw metal, old car parts, and even a sink. And then there were shapes that clearly *had* been furniture at some point but couldn't really be recognized anymore.

It was eerie, but not for the reason I expected. It wasn't that I felt like a ghost was about to jump out at me (though I wasn't ruling that out and I'd be happy when I wasn't the only one here anymore). It was that all this stuff had once been familiar. These things had all been in someone's home or used as an everyday part of their lives. But they had been thrown away. They were just left here to be forgotten.

With a *whump*, Nathaniel made the short leap from the fence slat to the ground. I was relieved to have him next to me.

"Okay," he whispered, awed, surveying the junkyard. "We did it. I can't believe we did it."

I was with him 100 percent.

"Okay, let's go," Nathaniel said. We began to walk forward. I heard a strange noise, then realized it was Nathaniel, whispering to himself.

"Here we are. Ghost hunting in unexpected conditions. Operation Ghosts. Or, Halloween Hijinks."

"What do you mean 'unexpected conditions'? Did you have expected ghost conditions?"

"I thought there'd be a haunted house," Nathaniel replied. "And chains. And maybe someone saying 'Oooooooh.'"

I let out something between a nervous laugh and a snort. It felt nice to talk. It reminded me that this was just me and Nathaniel, that we were only next door. We were close to the everyday world.

But as we walked deeper and deeper into the junkyard, it felt harder to remember that.

All around us, heaps of metal rose like small mountains and ridges.

Pieces of wire and pipes reached toward us like fingers. Sometimes, in the flashlight beam I could recognize a ripped sofa or rusted, jagged piece of sink piping.

But other times, the light threw the piles into jangling shadow, making them look like they were from another world, one where they breathed and moved on their own.

Somehow, it was colder in the junkyard. Somehow, the night felt thicker, like there was mist in the air.

My hand shook, and my flashlight beam fluttered in response.

But Nathaniel's beam was steady. In fact, for someone who's scared of ghosts, he seemed very okay. Excited even.

"So," I squeaked out, desperate to break the creepy quiet. "What are we looking for exactly? I mean, other than a ghost popping out of thin air?"

"Well," Nathaniel said, looking around. "We might

find a clue. Evidence of the supernatural. Something that seems off. Or a spot that feels especially cold, or where all of a sudden you get a weird or bad feeling. Things like that."

I had a lot of bad feelings at the moment but didn't think that was the clue Nathaniel was looking for.

"Another question," I said, to take my mind off a looming old refrigerator, covered in dirt and rust. "What are ghosts exactly? Like, could I touch a ghost? Or could a ghost just hop on a plane and move somewhere else?"

"It's really interesting," Nathaniel said, clearly in his element, "there are lots of different opinions on ghosts. Some say ghosts are only kept here because of an unresolved connection to something. So they might be tied to a place, or a house, or an object."

"Huh," I said, thinking about how terrifying a haunted toaster would be. Then something else occurred to me.

"Can a ghost be connected to a person?"

"Some people think so," Nathaniel said. "But not in a possession kind of way. More like, they might attach to the person, and follow them around. Like they might torment them, or urge them on."

"Wow," I said. "That sounds stressful."

"Yeah," Nathaniel said. "And then other people think that ghosts are more like the memory of a place. So when something bad or intense happens, other people may forget, but the places don't. The places hold those feelings. It's like the memory, or the feeling, of whatever happened is so strong that it won't stay down. And then, ghosts."

"That kind of makes sense," I said, listening to my feet crunch on the rocky dirt. "It's still stressful, but I can see how that would happen."

"But then other people say that ghosts are just versions of dead people made of ectoplasm."

"What's ectoplasm?"

"Oh, it's SO COOL, it's . . ."

Nathaniel launched into a very technical description of what I think can be best described as "ghostly goo." Focusing on his voice helped me relax.

As I got used to the junkyard, it didn't lose any of its scariness. But as we walked, I realized that it was also kind of fascinating. The heaps in the junkyard felt like clues to the past. I wondered when the old-fashioned car parts were used, and why that rusty oven was painted lime green. I wondered who had sat on that moldy sofa frame, and how long it had taken for grass to sprout up in that tire.

Every once in a while, we could hear the voices of trick-or-treaters down the road, laughing and sugar high. A few, terrifying times, we had to turn off our flashlights just so no one saw any light and came to investigate.

Finally, we found what we were looking for.

The spot where the firefighters had been was still surrounded by caution tape. You could see where bits of metal had been scorched.

"It was just a fluke fire," the firefighters had said.

Unless it wasn't a fluke. Unless *this* was where it happened, all those years ago, and the fire somehow started again, like it was stuck in a nightmarish, repeating loop.

I tried to imagine what this must have looked like, back when the circus was here. This whole stretch would have been a clear field, with no junk in sight. Was I standing on the spot where the fire broke out?

Was Maudie here, buried right under my feet?

All of a sudden, I had a strange urge.

"Maudie," I called out, keeping my voice low. "Maudie, are you there? Can you hear me?"

Nathaniel's eyes darted around nervously.

We both held our breath.

"Maudie," I started again, "are you—"

BANG.

I dropped my flashlight.

"WHAT WAS THAT?!" Nathaniel wielded his flashlight like a sword, trying to find the source.

BANG. We heard it again, from the darkness of one of the scorched piles.

"Maudie?" I whispered, my voice a shake.

Bang, bang, bang, BANG! The sound intensified, like it was coming toward me. I leapt back—

"Hya!!" With a yell, Nathaniel tossed his saltshaker.

It hit metal with a metallic *thump*.

Nathaniel shined his flashlight on the spot.

It was just an old car. There was one final *bang!* and then a mouse—who had clearly been chewing and banging under the hood—skittered across it, frightened by the light.

There was nothing there.

"Thanks," I said to Nathaniel, when I'd caught my breath.

"No problem," he said, also sounding shaken. "Except now I have to explain to my parents where the saltshaker went, but that's for tomorrow."

I nodded.

"Sorry," Nathaniel said, putting his hands on his thighs like he was getting his balance. "I just need a sec. That was TERRIFYING."

He put his hand back to lean against a tarp-covered heap.

And fell through.

"Nathaniel!" I screamed, as he disappeared into the side of the pile. "Are you—"

"Look what I found!" Nathaniel said, popping his head out, sounding very okay. Excited even.

I peered around.

The tarp was hanging like a curtain.

Through it was a small, sheltered area, like someone had carved a tiny cave in the side of one of the junk piles. An old car hood and decayed patio umbrella held the tarp up in place.

I walked in. The shelter was just tall enough for us—anyone else would have to stoop.

There were old sofa cushions, sprouting metal in some places, laid out for sitting, and there was cardboard on the ground, like flooring. There was a blanket in the corner.

Someone had been there. Recently.

"We should go," I said.

"But," Nathaniel protested, gesturing at his find.

"This isn't a ghost," I said. "This is something human. Come on." I stepped out of the shelter.

And nearly tripped over something on the ground, right at my feet.

I swear it hadn't been there before, though I'd been in such a panic to get to Nathaniel, that maybe I'd missed it? Maybe we both had?

It was old, I could tell that from looking at it. Like *old*, old. Like so old that the cloth looked like old paper that was curling up and fragmenting at the edges.

"Nathaniel," I whispered.

"Is that . . . ?" He trailed off, like he couldn't bring himself to say it.

I picked it up.

It was a hat.

An old black top hat.

I'd seen a hat just like this, in this very field.

On the head of Thomas Childers.

"It could be a coincidence, right?" I asked.

Then, in the distance, we heard one loud, sharp bark.

Nathaniel and I looked at each other with wide, terrified eyes.

"Let's get out of here," I said.

I didn't need to hear his reply to know that Nathaniel agreed with me. We raced out, back the way we had come.

We skidded to a halt at the fence, and I was about to tell Nathaniel to climb up first, when he paused.

"Wait, what's that?" he asked. He shined his flashlight down. Something glinted, the top just visible in the dirt. "Look, it's a marble, like in your dream!" Nathaniel said. "I'll get it."

"Wait, don't!" I said. "The dirt has sharp stuff in it, you'll hurt—"

But Nathaniel was already scooping his hand in.

"It's just a patch of— OW!"

He pulled his hand up.

"Nathaniel!" I said.

"It's fine," he said, dazed, examining his hand. "I think it was a piece of glass. It didn't really get me, thank goodness, because I faint at the sight of b—"

"Uh, Nathaniel," I said.

Because even without the flashlight, I could see blood on his hand.

A lot of blood.

I ran toward him.

CHAPTER 15

THE JUNKYARD STRIKES BACK

Chess is a series of moves and countermoves. You explore, you go into enemy territory, then they strike back.

Or at least, these are the cardinal rules of chess, according to Nathaniel.

We played a lot of chess those next two weeks. Or really, Nathaniel played and I just forgot what the pieces do and found new and creative ways to lose.

Nathaniel was grounded. He was fine, but grounded.

Because apparently when you get a cut, even minor (which thankfully his was), it's really important to know what cut you, and how sanitary it was.

So Nathaniel had to admit that he'd been in the old junkyard, and that he'd been cut by mystery metal that looked a little rusty. So then, a cut turned into an ER visit and a tetanus shot.

And then the grounding.

I felt TERRIBLE.

Especially because I wasn't punished much at all.

Uncle Ray sat me down and told me he understood that I wanted to explore, but the junkyard was dangerous and off-limits. I agreed, and that was it.

My mom didn't say a word about it.

Nathaniel told his parents it was all his idea, and they believed him. So I was allowed to visit, even while he was grounded, on the condition that we did schoolwork, with no TV, no computer time, and definitely no ghost research.

Hence the chess, once our homework was done.

I was in the process of losing particularly badly (which is saying something), when Nathaniel paused, tilting his head to listen at the door. Once he was sure his parents weren't outside, he turned back to me and spoke quietly.

"Okay, I've been thinking, and I have a new theory."

"Are you sure?" I asked. "I don't want you to get into any more trouble. It's bad enough that you got hurt."

"I'm totally fine!" Nathaniel said, holding up his hand and pointing at the bandage. "I could probably take this off right now, if my parents wouldn't get upset. Besides, I had fun. It was an ADVENTURE!"

I couldn't help but smile, even though I was still worried. Nathaniel certainly had a way of making *anything* seem exciting.

"So here's my theory," he said, leaning in. "I don't think it's Maudie's ghost that's causing all the damage."

"So . . . you don't think there's a ghost after all?" I asked.

"No, I think there are *definitely* ghosts," he said. "But remember what you said, about the fire? How it was like it was repeating on a loop?"

"Yeah." I nodded.

"Well, that's just it! I think you're being caught up in a loop. Like the past is repeating. Every time you've seen Maudie, it's like she's asking for help. And the thing she'd need help with, or need to escape is—"

"Thomas Childers," I said, finishing the sentence for him.

As I did, it all clicked. It made perfect sense.

"Yeah," Nathaniel said. "Exactly. He seems like a scary guy. And just the sort of person who wouldn't be able to let something like this go. Even in death. It also explains why his hat was there, and how the hat is so well-preserved. Connections to a ghost can do that."

We were silent for a moment. I wondered how it was possible for a feeling of impending doom to somehow get a lot worse.

"Okay, but there is good news," Nathaniel said. "Really. See, not much is known about animal ghosts. That's why reaching Maudie might be tricky. But

Thomas Childers is a person. There's TONS of research on how to summon and deal with human ghosts. Now that we know who we're looking for, we can do something about it."

"But you're grounded," I said. "I can try researching at the library on my own, but you're the ghost expert."

"Not to worry." Nathaniel grinned.

Inside Nathaniel's closet, where you'd expect clothes to be hanging, were books.

I mean wall-to-wall shelves of books.

"Is this every ghost book ever published?" I asked.

"No," he said. "Trust me, I have a HUGE wish list."

He pulled out the books he thought would help the most.

"Where did you get these? Weren't they expensive?" It felt a little rude to ask, but seriously—some of these books were enormous and *fancy*, like bound-in-hardcover-with-gold-writing-on-the-titles fancy.

"My Zayde used to give me Hanukkah money every year," Nathaniel said, nodding toward a photo that I hadn't noticed on his desk. "And he used to give us money for every straight-A report card."

"Wow, that's nice," I said, walking over to look at the

photo. Nathaniel's Zayde was wearing a white lab coat in the photo and was standing next to a young man who I realized, with a start, was Nathaniel's dad, but muuuuch younger (and with hair).

"Yeah," Nathaniel said, and it took me a moment to realize he sounded kind of sad. "He died last summer."

"Oh, Nathaniel," I said, putting the photo down. "I'm sorry. I shouldn't have brought it up."

"No, it's okay," Nathaniel said. "He was sick, so it wasn't a surprise, but . . ." He looked at his feet.

"Well, I just wish that he'd been around for all this, you know? For Maudie, and everything we're finding out. He was a doctor, just like his dad, and my dad. He was . . . kind of intense. He always talked about how you needed a job that would always be useful. And well, last year I wasn't doing that well in school, and he told me I had to do better and make him proud."

Nathaniel paused. Sadness seemed to seep through him, like in that one moment, his whole body was showing me what his words couldn't.

"And I was just in a bad mood that day and I got mad, because I'm not like my brothers and sisters, and I'm not as good at science and math and school as they are. So I just walked out. And I didn't realize just how sick he was—the next time I saw him, he was in the hospital, and he couldn't really talk . . ." He trailed off, but then took a deep breath and looked at me resolutely.

"That's why this is so important," he said. "I WILL make a difference. I'll prove that ghosts are real, once and for all. I'll make him proud, just like he wanted me to."

"It sounds like he loved you a lot, Nathaniel," I said gently, hoping that it was the right thing to say. "I don't think you had to prove anything to him."

Nathaniel shrugged.

"Thanks," he said. He sniffled. "Well, anyway. I used my Hanukkah money from him to buy ghost books, so there's a lot we can look through . . ."

He was changing the subject, which I knew something about.

And I thought there was probably a lot more we should talk about. But he didn't want to, and I also know something about that.

So I followed Nathaniel's lead, grabbed a book, and got to work.

That night, I couldn't get chess out of my head for some reason.

Move, countermove.

Nathaniel was right, I was sure of it. In all the accounts, Maudie was gentle and kind. She was asking for help, or trying to protect us. It was Childers who couldn't let go, who was holding on and seeking revenge.

Move, countermove.

I couldn't stop thinking about it.

I didn't figure out why until I fell asleep.

Because we were on to Thomas Childers. We'd gone into his territory. I had his top hat on my shelf.

We'd made a move.

And now, Childers would countermove.

In my dream, Maudie was standing there, rooted to the ground. And there was a tall man in a top hat, and he lifted an arm and there was an awful, ugly metal hook.

"NO!" I yelled. "Leave her alone!"

But I couldn't move, and he brought the hook down, and she screamed, and he lifted his arm again and kept hitting and hitting as I yelled "STOP!" but couldn't stop it.

"LEAVE HER ALONE!" I screamed, tasting my own tears and snot.

He raised the bullhook again, but this time coming toward me . . .

And then the floor broke apart, and I was floating away from them both, reaching for Maudie but not

122

able to grab her. And a quiet, faraway voice began to sing, slowly:

"Hush little baby . . ."

"Leave her alone," I sobbed again.

"Don't say a word . . . ," sang the voice.

I looked around to find it—maybe the voice could help me?

And then, as Maudie disappeared into darkness, I realized who it was.

"Mama's gonna buy you a mockingbird . . . ," sang the faraway, sad voice. It was *CeCe's* voice.

"You leave my family alone, Thomas Childers!" I yelled into the dark. "You leave CeCe alone!"

"CeCe!" I woke myself up, talking in my sleep.

It was morning, and I was in a kitchen chair, with a pillow stuck weirdly under my neck.

I got up, hoping to make it upstairs before anyone came out and saw me.

I made it to the bottom of the stairs, and that's when I glanced out the front window. Then I screamed.

Sometime in the night, Uncle Ray's mailbox had been destroyed.

By someone wielding something large and heavy.

Like an iron bullhook.

CHAPTER 16

TICK, TICK ... BOOM?

"I don't understand it," Uncle Ray said mournfully, picking up the pieces of his mailbox. "What could have happened?"

"It could be a moose," my mom suggested from the doorway.

"Or a monster," CeCe whispered.

I didn't say anything. How could I?

No one would believe me.

Danger, I felt, thrumming beneath my skin.

"Well, Carol will be here soon," Uncle Ray said. "I'll cover it with a tarp. Maybe she won't notice?" he added hopefully.

I grimaced, and even my mom made a face. There was little chance of that.

"What's up with the mailbox?" Auntie Carol asked as soon as she'd sat down.

"Oh, I just wanted a change," Uncle Ray said, too casually, handing her a mug of tea.

"Plus the monster," CeCe added helpfully as she offered the plate of apple-and-carrot muffins to Auntie

Carol. "The stomping moose monster. I think it hates the mailbox."

Uncle Ray closed his eyes, my mom sighed, and I bit back a half-laughing, half-choking sound, as CeCe blinked on obliviously.

"AY-YAH," Auntie Carol rounded on Uncle Ray, and I swear he shrank a few inches in his seat. "I told you, you shouldn't live here!" she said, jabbing him with her finger.

"The animals aren't so bad," my mom jumped in, surprising us all. "I think this is just a fluke."

"Yeah—" I started. But Auntie Carol cut me off.

"Oh, for heaven's sakes, girls, it's not animals," she said curtly. "It's people. You should live in the city, Ray. More Chinese people, less risk like this."

I sat back, startled. Whatever I'd expected Auntie Carol to say, it wasn't *that*.

"It's not like—" Uncle Ray started.

"Oh, the yard of one of the only Chinese families in town is destroyed, and you think it's an accident? Grow up, little brother, stop seeing the world through your rose-colored hippie glasses."

Uncle Ray crossed his arms resolutely.

"I believe people are good," he said.

"And what do they believe about you, huh?"

Uncle Ray didn't know what to say to that. And

125

I didn't either. Because it wasn't people—it was Thomas Childers. But was what Auntie Carol said wrong?

I thought about the looks I got on the first day, the kid who pulled his eyes back, the man who didn't believe I lived in New Warren.

What if Auntie Carol was right?

Danger, said the beat in my ears.

Auntie Carol left early that day. Uncle Ray went into the kitchen and started banging pots and pans as he made lunch. CeCe went upstairs, and my mom went into the kitchen to help Uncle Ray.

And me?

I couldn't relax.

Danger, my brain said.

Nathaniel's grounding was just about over, so his parents let me talk to him that afternoon when I called. I told him about the mailbox and felt a catch in my throat that wouldn't seem to let go.

Danger.

"I promise, we'll figure this out, Mo," he said. "I'll come in Monday with a plan."

"Thanks," I whispered.

But inside, all I could feel was the fast, unrelenting beat inside me.

Danger.

In the kitchen, Uncle Ray had announced we were having a "brunch lunch" and was whipping up eggs and tofurkey bacon.

My mom was helping and they were chatting happily, but—

"Mom, careful! Don't touch the raw eggs, you'll get sick!" I said.

"Uncle Ray, do those knives really need to be that sharp? And you're leaving the toaster oven *on* while you're at the other counter?"

Danger, danger, danger, my insides sirened.

"Mo," Uncle Ray said with a tired-sounding sigh. "You gotta relax. Here, why don't you sit down. I'll make you some toast and—"

"NO," I said. And as I did, even *I* could tell how weirdly upset about it I was.

"I'll have cereal," I said.

I poured some into a bowl, added milk, and stormed out of the kitchen.

"She's getting into those teen years," I heard my mom say as I left.

I wanted to shout at them. I wanted to scream: "THAT'S NOT IT AT ALL, I'M TRYING TO KEEP YOU SAFE."

But instead, I just stomped upstairs.

"Look, they're having a party," CeCe said, gesturing

to her stuffed animals, which were all on the floor. "Come and play with me, Mo!"

I took a deep breath and put my cereal bowl down on my bookshelf.

"I can't play, CeCe," I said. "But I need to talk to you." I sat cross-legged on the floor across from her. "This is very important—did you have any bad dreams last night?"

"No," CeCe said with a small frown. "Did you?"

"CeCe, this is SERIOUS," I said. "Did you have any bad or weird dreams last night?!"

"I said 'no,'" CeCe said. "I didn't. Did you?"

"Okay, phew," I said. "But listen to me. If you hear circus music, don't follow it."

"You're weird sometimes, Mo," CeCe said. "Are you going to play or not?" She held out a toy.

"I'm busy," I said shortly.

"You're weird and also MEAN," CeCe declared. And she stormed downstairs. Had I done a good enough job? Was she telling the truth? Was she safe from whatever was in my dreams?

Danger.

It was in my body, it was all I could see, it was the pulse in my ears, and it sat on my chest. And no one understood.

From downstairs I could hear my mom and Uncle

Ray and CeCe, talking and going on as if they didn't have a worry in the world.

All of a sudden, I wasn't just worried, I was MAD.

Why did *I* have to deal with all of this?

Why was it all up to *me*?

I reached for my cereal, where I'd set it down on my bookshelf, but instead my fingers hit the top hat.

The top hat that, at that moment, seemed to laugh at me, seemed to embody *everything* that was weird and creepy and going wrong and DANGEROUS.

And suddenly, I couldn't stand it anymore.

Without thinking, without remembering how old and fragile it was, or that it was our one piece of evidence that ghosts might exist, I picked it up and threw it with all my might.

It hit the bedroom wall with a *WHUMPH*.

And the danger I'd been worried about all along came spilling out.

CHAPTER 17

A CLUE, A MAP, A NEW IDEA

It took a minute for my eyes to make sense of it.

When the top hat hit the wall, something popped out.

I tiptoed toward it, like I was worried it might come alive.

There was a letter—stuffed into the lining of the hat. I hadn't been able to see it before, but when I'd thrown it, it must have come loose.

I drew it out with shaking hands.

It was crumpled, and the ink was faded brown, but I could still read it. On one side, it said:

Ralph Childers
Millbrook Lane
New Warren

I unfolded it, and in the same long spindly script. It read:

Father,

Our performance is scheduled for the thirtieth

of March. Enclosed is a ticket. I hope you will approve of what your son has made of himself.

—Thomas

And alongside the letter was a small rectangular piece of yellowed paper, that read:

FLYING BROTHERS CIRCUS: ADMIT ONE.

Several things hit me at once.

First: This was it! Confirmation. This hat WAS connected to Thomas Childers—otherwise why would a letter like this be inside it, with a circus ticket no less? *This* was the clue Nathaniel had been talking about.

The second fact took another moment to hit me. But when it did, it hit hard.

The letter was addressed to an unspecified house on Millbrook Lane.

A lane I knew well, because I was on Millbrook Lane right now.

Thomas Childers, and his whole family, were connected to this very street.

And I had to find out how.

For once, I didn't need to call Nathaniel. I knew *exactly* what to do.

I emptied one of my school folders, put the letter, envelope, and ticket inside, and ran down the stairs.

"Is it okay if I go to the library?" I asked, peering into the kitchen, where my mom, Uncle Ray, and CeCe sat eating. My cheeks got red, as I remembered how rude I'd been. "Uh, I mean, if that's okay, of course . . . ," I stuttered.

"Of course," my mom said.

I smiled, waved, and ran out of the house.

I made it to the library in record time. *Please be here, please be here, please be here*, I thought, scanning the archive room. And then—

"Lavender!" I called.

"Hey, Mo!" She smiled at me. She was as cool as ever, in a dark blue jumpsuit and long yellow sweater, with bright yellow shoes to match.

"How's your research going?"

"Actually," I said, drawing out the folder. "I need your help."

"Wow, kid," Lavender said for the third time, holding the letter up to the light. "This is a great find. You know, Lincoln used to keep letters in the brim of his top hat too. Here . . ."

She turned back, rummaged in her desk, and drew out a beige envelope.

"Keep it in there. These are archival folders. They're acid free, and won't degrade paper. You actually might want to wear gloves if you're going to handle these a lot too, but we can talk about that later.

"So," she said, placing the letter and ticket gently in the new folder. "What are you trying to figure out?"

"Well," I said slowly, gauging just how much I could tell her. "I'm really interested in Thomas Childers, the one with the circus. And Ralph Childers must have been his dad, right? And Millbrook Lane is where I'm living. So, I guess, I want to figure out the connection. Is the Childers house still there? And what was up between the two of them?"

"Great questions," Lavender said. "I can at least help with one of them. I've been doing some digging and asking around, ever since I ran into you and your friend. You got me curious. Here, come with me," she said, her yellow shoes already in motion.

I followed her into the main library rotunda. It was the oldest, grandest part of the building, with marble columns reaching up to a second-story balcony. The base of the balcony had shelves carved into it, and each had a marble bust of a face resting in it.

"These are all the founders and prominent members of New Warren," Lavender said. "And that"—she pointed—"is Thomas Childers's grandfather, P. Edward Childers, one of the founders of New Warren."

I looked up at the bust. I recognized him, and I didn't think it was my imagination. I'd seen the very same eyes, and the same face shape, in the photo at town hall. Thomas Childers looked a lot like his grandfather.

"Wow," I said, looking up at the stern statue. "He seems intense."

"Well, he probably was," Lavender said. "Or at least, he was very driven. He bought up a lot of land in New Warren and made a lot of money. But his son lost it all."

"Wait, Ralph Childers? The one who the letter is addressed to?"

"Exactly," Lavender said. "He was a gambler, and he drank, and he pretty much whittled his father's estate away. Back then, that would have been seen as the ultimate disgrace—this once venerated family, now with almost nothing."

"So that's why the book said their family fortunes were reduced. And Thomas Childers went into the circus to make back the money his dad had lost."

"Yes, to rebuild his family fortune, and to rebuild his family name, in a sense. Again, back then, status and what people knew about you was everything."

"And I mean, judging by that letter, he and his dad maybe didn't get along," I added.

"I think you're right," she said. "I don't think his dad was a very nice man."

"But," I said, processing it all. "So *his* dad wasn't very nice, and did not-great things, sure. But then *he* responded by not being very nice either! Look what he did to Maudie!" I crossed my arms. "I wish people were less complicated."

"It's a challenge," Lavender said. "As historians, we have to look at people in all their flaws and complexities."

I stared up at the stern face of P. Edward Childers.

"So," I said, thinking about this family, and all the versions of their faces I'd seen around town. "How come we have all these history exhibits in New Warren, and all these brochures with Maudie the elephant and photos of Thomas Childers, but no one mentions any of this? Shouldn't this be part of the history too? And shouldn't how Thomas Childers treated Maudie and other people be part of the history?"

"Spot on, Mo," Lavender said. "It should be, but it gets hidden. That's what happens. People try to clean up history. Just like no one talks about the native peoples whose lands were stolen to create New Warren. Or the fact that town hall was built by enslaved people, and that a great deal of New Warren's wealth was made possible by enslaved labor."

"Oh," I said. "I had no idea."

"Yeah, these things get erased," Lavender said.

"You know what else—you know how New Warren was an industrial center in the mid-1900s, and made all this money from factories?"

I nodded—I'd heard about this in school.

"Well, that industry almost never happened. There was a strike at one of the early shoe factories down the road, which almost killed the business. But guess who was brought in and helped it thrive?"

"Who?" I asked.

"Chinese workers," she said. "Then, of course, even after they saved the factory and came up with technological innovations to help it run more smoothly, they were still paid less than white workers, and ultimately, were driven out of town."

"What? Really?" I asked.

"Yeah," Lavender said. "Chinese laborers have been in America since the Revolutionary War. But that's never taught in history."

I realized, with surprise, that my heart was pounding. I was . . . mad. But a different kind of mad than earlier that day.

"I can't believe this!" I said. "How can we never

have learned any of this in school?! How can we take field trips to town hall, and not learn who built it?" I was ranting, but I didn't care. "And so, when people are surprised I'm from here, which happens *all the time*—"

"You tell them your ancestors made this place possible," Lavender said, pounding her fist in her palm.

She didn't mind that I was mad. She didn't tell me to "just relax." She understood.

"Thanks, Lavender," I said, quieter now. "Sometimes this town is . . . I dunno . . ."

"Hard? Small-minded? Full of microaggressions, like someone assuming you're not from America?"

"Yeah." I nodded. "Pretty much."

"We've got each other," she said. "And things can change. I'm working right now to start a museum, here in New Warren, that honors the Black Americans who helped create this town."

"That's incredible," I said with a sigh. "Can I work there when I'm old enough?"

"Uh, I'm going to hold you to that," she said with a smile.

I grinned back, then something occurred to me.

"You know," I said, "you should meet my Uncle Ray. He's big into music, and he's been telling me about singers like Sister Rosetta Tharpe, and Chuck Berry, and Little Richard, who pretty much made rock music possible. But then white singers and producers stole their songs and their styles, and they didn't get any credit for it, or money. It's just like what you're saying with history! I bet he'd love to help with your museum."

"Why thank you, Mo," she said. "I'd love that. Now, as much as I could talk about history all day, I know you had another research question. I don't know anything about the Childers house, but I know someone who can help. Have you ever been to the reserved archives room? The one where we keep the super-old stuff?"

"No!" I said. "That sounds so cool!"

"Well, prepare to wear gloves, kid," she said with a laugh. "And absolutely NO water or gum allowed, and don't even think about bringing a pen in there . . ."

I didn't leave the library until closing. When I did, I went straight to Nathaniel's door.

Nathaniel answered the bell.

"Mo! Is everything okay?"

"I know where he is," I said. "I know how to get rid of Childers, once and for all."

"How?" he asked.

I told him. He was torn between total terror and being kind of excited, just like I knew he'd be.

Because this story was about to have a real live haunted house.

CHAPTER 18

HAUNTED ANCESTRAL FAMILY ESTATES ARE AS TERRIFYING AS YOU WOULD EXPECT

It was getting cold.

Uncle Ray was talking about his tofurkey, even though things between him and Auntie Carol were frosty, so I didn't know how well any family holiday gatherings would go.

I didn't want to think about Thanksgiving, or the fact that winter break was approaching. There was no way to think about holidays without bringing up memories of holidays past.

But luckily, I had a distraction.

Nathaniel had found an exorcism.

"There are tons of different kinds of exorcisms," Nathaniel explained during Library Lunch Club that week. "But I've found the best because it's in a language I can read and there's no blood involved."

"I'm sorry, what?" I asked, staring at him.

"Nothing you need to know about," Nathaniel said lightly. "And I think I can get a lot of the supplies . . ."

I tried to focus and listen, but it was hard over the pounding in my ears. Sneaking into the junkyard had been scary enough. But it was right next door. If anything had happened, we could have screamed and someone would have heard us.

But a haunted house? In the middle of the woods?

Let's just say, my terror levels had gone from "Alert!" to "ABANDON THIS SHIP RIGHT NOW."

But I took a deep breath, and reminded myself that this wasn't for me. This was for Maudie. And it was to keep my family safe.

I tuned back in to the moment just as Nathaniel was saying, in a *very* loud voice, "I think I have most of the supplies at my house. We have all this stuff for the holidays. So even though I don't know how to get holy water, we can just use my dad's Manischewitz instead! It's religious so it should work, and that ghost won't know what hit him when we storm right into the old Childers house—"

"Nathaniel!" I hissed. "Keep your voice down. This is a secret, remember?"

"Sorry," Nathaniel whispered. "I just get excited!"

"I know," I said. "But we have to be careful, okay? We can't have anything going wrong again. This can't be like the junkyard."

"Gotcha," Nathaniel said. "Anyway," he went on, still whispering but clearly humming with excitement, "I've figured out the ceremony we'll use. It's Latin, and it has a very specific order, but also uses things we can get, like candles and chalk. But I also have a backup in case it doesn't work. It's FASCINATING. The language of an exorcism basically banishes the spirit. But there are lots of different kinds of exorcisms from different cultures. In some, you cast a spirit out, but in others you're actually offering to help it too. Really, I think it's the intentions that matter, more than the words. We acknowledge the ghost, then invite it to move on. I have the rituals from three different traditions, so if one doesn't work, we'll try the next . . ."

"Nathaniel!" I whispered.

His voice had risen with every sentence, until he was speaking in his normal, very-easy-to-overhear way.

"This all sounds great," I said, even as my stomach twisted in protest, because it actually sounded very uncertain and terrifying. "But why don't we write it down, instead of talking. That way, no one can overhear us?"

"Oh, great idea!" Nathaniel said in his normal voice, reaching for his notebook.

So that's what we did.

Over the next few days, we passed our notes back

and forth. Nathaniel was in charge of the steps of the ceremony and supplies, and I contributed salt from Uncle Ray's house (though I put it in a bag, rather than the saltshaker, in case we had a repeat of the junkyard).

I was in charge of the map and drew our route— down an old path behind Uncle Ray's house, which would take us through the woods, and lead us right to the house.

We were in Library Lunch Club toward the end of the third week in November, when we were finally ready.

I looked over our notes one more time.

"Okay. We'll go next week, just before break. We have everything we need."

"Yeah," Nathaniel said. "Can you believe it? One more week and we'll finally have PROOF."

My stomach felt sour at the thought, but Nathaniel sounded, if anything, *excited*.

"Nathaniel," I said. "This isn't a game—this is more dangerous than the junkyard, and you got hurt there. Promise me you're taking this seriously."

"Of course!" Nathaniel chirped. But then he saw my face. He took a breath and looked at me steadily. "I am, I promise," he said. "Trust me, Mo. We got this."

And even though I'd had my doubts, and even though I was still terrified about what we were planning to do, I realized that deep down, I believed him.

It was a kind of surprising feeling.

Look at everything he'd done for me.

And I knew that for him, this was a BIG deal. This was his chance to prove that he was serious—to know that his Zayde would have been proud of him. Of course he was excited.

"You're right," I said with a smile. "We can do this. Now." I handed him our notes. "Take this, memorize it, destroy the evidence when you're done."

"Will do," Nathaniel said, nodding seriously.

Later that day, in history, I saw him looking through the notes and mouthing to himself. At the end of class, he ripped them up, put them in the recycling, and gave me a thumbs-up.

It wasn't perfect stealth, but it was solid for Nathaniel.

The night before we set our plan in motion, I couldn't sleep.

I lay in bed, staring at the closet ceiling, worry roiling in my belly.

Were we really going to do this? Could I even bring

myself to walk into so much danger? What if something went wrong? What if Nathaniel's rituals weren't enough? What if I just stayed here in the safety of my house and never said the word "ghost" again?

I turned one way, then the other. I fluffed my pillow, and then flattened it, and fluffed it again.

Then I sat up. I meant to get a book to read and distract my panicking brain, but instead, I found my fingers closing over the blue marble that I kept on top of the bookcase.

I lay back down and turned the marble between my fingers again and again.

Maudie had given this to me. She'd come to me. She'd asked for my help after being left behind, with no one to help her, no one to even remember she was there.

I fell asleep with the marble in my hand, and a resolve.

Was I terrified beyond words? Yes.

But I was going to do this. For Maudie.

The next night, Nathaniel came over before dinner.

Act casual, I told myself.

"Hi, Nathaniel!" I said as I opened the door. "So

great you could come over for a sleepover!" I realized that my voice was a little too loud and bright, but look, YOU try acting when you're about to break every rule to confront an angry evil ghost in a real live haunted house.

"Uh, thanks for inviting me. For a sleepover," Nathaniel said.

He was actually a mildly better actor than I am—he just channeled his nerves by being more jittery and bouncy than ever.

"Check out my supplies, Mo!" Nathaniel whispered, shifting from foot to foot, plopping his overnight bag down on the couch. "I brought glowsticks in case we need to scatter them around for light in the woods. I brought Hanukkah candles for the ceremony, and chalk, and my dad's tallis because religious objects always help, and—"

"Shhh! Nathaniel, CeCe might hear," I whispered. I nodded to the next room, where she was coloring. "We have to pretend like nothing is going on, remember? It's just a normal night."

"Right," Nathaniel whispered back. "Sorry."

"So, uh, about our science homework," I said loudly, leading Nathaniel into the other room, where he said hi to CeCe. I looked at her face carefully. I didn't think she'd heard anything. She's five, and I don't think five is really an age for keeping secrets, or being subtle about anything.

Nathaniel, CeCe, and I helped Uncle Ray cook. I felt like, at any moment, Uncle Ray would know something was wrong. I worried I'd let something slip if I said too much, or that he'd just be able to read our plan all over my guilty, terrified face. So I stayed mostly quiet. But Nathaniel entertained CeCe with funny stories about his siblings, and I don't think anyone noticed.

Nathaniel went to help CeCe wash her hands and I helped Uncle Ray bring out the serving bowls. I put the last bowls on the table just as Nathaniel and CeCe walked back into the kitchen, and I heard the end of their conversation.

"I want to help," I heard CeCe say.

"And you can," Nathaniel said. "Here's how . . ."

Then Uncle Ray called me in to grab a plate, and I didn't hear what came after that.

When I came back in, CeCe and Nathaniel were giggling about something.

"Pinkie promise?" CeCe asked.

"Pinkie promise," Nathaniel said with a smile.

"What was that about?" I asked, when Uncle Ray was helping CeCe cut her food, and Nathaniel and I were filling our plates at the kitchen counter.

"Oh, it's just a thing I used to do with my brothers

and sisters. I'm the youngest too, you know. So I gave CeCe a 'little sister responsibility.' It's something Zayde taught me. He was a youngest brother too, and he said we youngests had to stick together." Nathaniel smiled. "Basically, I gave her a job. It always made me feel really cool and useful when I was a kid."

"Huh," I said. I looked over at CeCe. She was insisting that she cut her own food, so Uncle Ray was supervising while she used the sharper knife.

And she looked really happy about it. And capable.

It was something to consider. For later.

First, of course, I had to survive dinner. I wasn't sure if the millions of butterflies zooming around in my stomach left any room for food. But hunger won out over fear. Then we watched a movie, which somehow felt like a millisecond and an eternity all at the same time.

Nathaniel slept on the foldout couch downstairs. I went upstairs to my closet, but I didn't fall asleep. How could I?

I didn't even change into my pajamas. I just lay there, in the dark, staring at the glow-in-the-dark stars on my ceiling and tapping my fingers against the blue marble in my hand. Every once in a while, I reminded myself to breathe. Every two minutes, I checked the clock.

Finally, at 11:00 on the dot, I crept downstairs to find Nathaniel already in his fleece jacket, ready to go.

Nathaniel and I had studied the maps Lavender and the head archivist, Larry, helped us find. They had shown that the old Childers house was located behind Uncle Ray's house, on an older version of Millbrook Lane that had been redrawn when the railroad tracks had cut through it. According to Larry, the old road should connect to the path where the now-abandoned railroad tracks stood.

So, we wound our way behind Uncle Ray's house following the weed-covered, splintering tracks.

Every rustle of branches in the dark made my stomach plunge like I was on a roller coaster. But following Nathaniel made it easier to keep going. He was pale, and I could see from the way his flashlight bounced that his hands were shaking. But he was strangely quiet and purposeful too. It was like every ounce of him was focused on what lay ahead.

Nathaniel spotted the old road first—a dirt path, overgrown but still visible, that veered off into the trees.

"Well, here goes nothing," Nathaniel sighed, and stepped in.

I paused.

The trees were thick and packed together, a dark mass of trunks and branches that looked like hands reaching for you. I felt panic swirl in my chest, so real that it was like an actual physical pressure.

I put my hand in my pocket, and wrapped it around Maudie's marble, which I'd tucked safely inside.

"I won't leave you behind," I whispered, feeling its light coolness. "I'll help you."

I took a deep breath and stepped into the dark.

I followed Nathaniel's lead and kept my beam trained straight in front of me so I could see where I was stepping and avoid tree roots and stones as the path dipped and rose around us.

I'd only been in darkness like this once before, darkness so thick that you could plunge into it like it was enveloping fog. It had been a camping trip, with S-Dad, when he and my mom had been dating for about a year. I was six, and I was scared of the dark.

But he'd shown me his headlamp and told me it was the strongest light in the world. He promised I could trust him. I followed him beyond our campsite, and he put the lamp on my head, and turned the light on, and I'll never forget that feeling, as the light cut through the dark, and the thing that had seemed so scary, so suffocating, opened up into a world of mist and grass and shades that were at once gray and so many other hues.

After that, he gave me the headlamp, so I could use it whenever I needed to.

After that, the dark hadn't seemed so scary.

Or at least, not for a long time.

Part of me wished I had the headlamp now.

Though the other part of me was glad I'd thrown it in the dumpster when we moved.

Nathaniel came to a sudden stop, bringing me back to the present of the night.

"Mo," he whispered, his voice trembling. "Is that . . . ?"

I followed his gaze. There, just at the top of the next curve in our path, was a dog-shaped figure, white and gleaming in the dark.

"Maudie!" I called.

She looked at us, for one brief moment over her shoulder, with eyes that were big and brown and kind and sad.

Then she darted off, down the path.

"Come on!" I said. Nathaniel and I scrabbled after her.

But she was waiting for us at the next bend. Too far ahead for us to catch her, but always close enough that we could follow.

"She's leading us," Nathaniel whispered, eyes huge in the light. "She knows where we're going—she's helping us."

So we followed her, creeping behind the ghost dog, following her through the wending trees and uneven stones, pausing a respectful distance when she stopped to sniff and, a few times, mark the trees.

Without saying a word, I think Nathaniel and I both felt the solemnity of the moment. We were following a ghost to fulfill its last wishes.

Which was weird, sure, but weren't most things in this town?

And weirder still, I realized as we moved into a thicker part of the woods, ducking under low branches and vaulting over fallen trunks, I wasn't scared. Or at least, not as scared as I'd thought I'd be.

Caught in the moonlight, Maudie glowed white and bright, like bottled lightning, flashing in the dark ahead of us.

In her glow, I noticed the way the rocks glittered, serene and calm in the light of my flashlight. Matching Maudie's slow, quiet pace, I noticed the insects and moths fluttering through the night, and imagined I could almost hear the sound in their wake as they flew by, it was so quiet.

I'd thought the woods would be terrifying.

But the thing is, the thing I'd learned and forgotten all those years ago was . . . it was kind of beautiful.

"Wow," I whispered.

"I know," Nathaniel whispered back, awed. "It's . . . not terrible."

"Not terrible at all," I said.

Then all of a sudden, the narrow path of the woods opened.

We found ourselves in a clearing, with overgrown grass and plants edging in, but not as big or deeply rooted as in the woods. And there, in the center of the clearing, was the house.

I caught a glimpse of Maudie's white tail as she disappeared around the side.

It was different than I'd thought it would be.

I mean, did it look like a haunted house? Yes.

It was old, with a pointed roof, crumbling shutters, and wooden slats that were covered in moss and grime. The windows were cracked, and some had no panes.

All of this I had sort of expected.

But I hadn't expected the house to look so *sad*.

It was old, crumbling, forgotten.

Somehow, that felt more upsetting than the ghost that probably waited inside.

"Well," Nathaniel said in a small voice. "I guess we should go in."

"Yeah," I whispered. I took a deep breath. "Okay," I said, nodding to the porch steps, trying to summon my courage. "One, two—"

"I can't believe you actually came here," a voice said from the porch.

I let out a yell, and Nathaniel fell backward in surprise.

There was a click of a flashlight, and then I saw his face.

"I'm impressed," Peter said from the porch. "I didn't know you two losers had it in you."

"H-how did—" Nathaniel spluttered.

But then we both saw it. In Peter's hand was a piece of paper, torn up, but taped back together. The notes Nathaniel had so obviously thrown away.

I closed my eyes and tried to stifle a screech of frustration.

"Sorry," Nathaniel whispered, wincing.

I knew I should say something back, but I worried if I did whatever came out wouldn't be nice. I turned to Peter instead.

"Why are you here, Peter?" I asked sharply.

"I wanted to see what you were doing. That's allowed."

"Well, now you've seen. But this is our business. Leave us alone."

"Maybe it's my business too," Peter said angrily. "Maybe you're trespassing and I want to know why." He paused. "Is this about the ghost?"

"You're only going to make fun of us if we tell you," I snapped.

"It's just." Peter stepped forward. "It's just that I have weird dreams sometimes."

I opened my mouth to respond but then—

Rustle.

Snap.

Creeeeak.

We all froze.

"It's the wind," I said.

"It came from the house," Peter said.

"Stop it, Peter," I said.

"I mean it! I'm not making fun! Something's in there!"

"You're a JERK," I said.

"Mo, c'mon," Nathaniel said. "He's serious."

I whirled on Nathaniel.

"So you're defending him now?" I asked. It was meaner than I'd meant it to be, but I was angry. How could Nathaniel be so careless?! "Why are you always doing that?" I asked. "Why do you always make excuses for him?"

"You think *he* cares what happens to me?" Peter said angrily. "He doesn't care. He made that super clear when he stopped hanging out with me, just because my parents split up."

I opened my mouth to respond, but no sound came out.

"That's not true!" Nathaniel cut in. "You started being really mean. I didn't want to do that. I didn't want any part in that."

"Oh, so last year I get to school and all of a sudden we're not friends anymore? And I'm the one who's mean?! You didn't come and talk to me, you didn't even ask how I was. No wonder no one likes you."

"You . . . you were friends?! And you didn't tell me?" I sputtered at Nathaniel, but it was Peter who answered.

"Yeah, and now you think you can just swoop in here with your weird family and UGH." Peter balled his hands up in frustration. "He's just going to drop you too!"

"Oh, now you're looking out for me, Mr. 'You-Live-with-a-Weird-Asian-Dude'?" I snapped. "You don't care about anyone but yourself." The volume was rising, inside my head and out. It was too much. How could Nathaniel not tell me these things, why was he hiding them, how could I trust him, why was he so incapable of being serious about things that mattered, why was Peter here, what would we do about Maudie, and Childers and why—

"Mo?"

The voice was soft, so low it felt like it belonged to another world. But it cut across our noise and yelling like a bell.

"CeCe?" I gasped.

She emerged from the woods, clutching one of Nathaniel's glowsticks for light, her shoes not quite tied.

"I thought I was lost, but then I heard you yelling," she said.

"What are you doing here?!" I demanded, racing over to her.

"I guessed," she said. "I knew you had a secret and I heard Nathaniel, so I asked him."

I glared at Nathaniel, and I don't think it was my imagination that Peter glared at him too.

"WHAT?" I said.

"Wait, no," Nathaniel said, putting up his hands. "I did NOT tell her."

"You said there was a secret plan, and my little sister responsibilities were to keep it secret. And I did! I didn't tell anyone!" she said proudly. "I just followed you with the glowstick you gave me to play with."

"Mo, I didn't think she'd foll—"

"THAT'S YOUR PROBLEM," I shouted, all the anger and frustration that had been building up inside me coming out in one awful wave. "You don't think! You just make things WORSE!"

"I've been helping you this whole time!" Nathaniel said, angry now too "I messed up, I know that, but I've been doing everything I can, even after you made fun of me and the ghosts, so—"

"You know what, you're right," I said back. "I don't need your help."

"Yes you do!" Nathaniel said. "You're scared of *toast* for crying out loud!! You definitely need *someone's* help!"

It felt like an actual slap. So I wanted to slap back.

"ME?!" I yelled. "You're afraid of GHOSTS but then you clearly love them! You don't know what danger is! Have you ever experienced anything really hard in your whole life?!"

Nathaniel took a step back.

I knew I was being mean; I knew I wasn't being fair. But I didn't care just then.

"You think *everything* is a game," I went on. "All I want is to be safe, to make everyone safe, and you promised you'd help and you lied. All you did was put us into even MORE danger." And then I said something that I knew I shouldn't, that I didn't mean at all. But I was SO angry. And it felt good to let that anger out at *someone*.

"No wonder Zayde couldn't be proud of you!" I said.

I turned away so I didn't have to see Nathaniel's face crumple.

"And you, Peter," I said, my voice low now. "I don't trust you at all. You're a BAD PERSON. You say you're sorry when you're not, you say you want to help, but you just make things worse. I'm done with both of you."

I scooped up CeCe, though she squirmed and protested that she could walk herself.

But I didn't listen.

I practically ran back through the woods, leaving Peter and Nathaniel behind me.

As I ran, my flashlight bouncing against the forest floor, I heard a bark.

In the distance, through the trees, I saw a white dog, outlined in the moonlight.

She was all alone.

She needed help.

But I couldn't help everyone.

I couldn't keep everyone safe.

I kept going, ignoring CeCe as she pounded at my back.

"Put me down, Mo!" she protested. "I want to help! I'm fine!"

But I didn't put her down until we broke through the trees, past the old tracks, into Uncle Ray's yard.

CeCe tumbled out of my arms.

"You're MEAN," CeCe shouted, pulling herself up and stomping her feet.

"*Quiet*," I hissed. "I'm trying to keep you safe."

"I was helping!" CeCe yelled.

"You *can't* help me! You don't understand anything!"

"I can too!" she said, her fists in tiny little balls at her waist. "You don't think I can do anything by myself, but I can, and I know things, and sometimes I—"

"What. Is. Going. On?!" Mom's voice boomed across the yard. She was standing at the porch door. For once, she looked like her old, alert self.

We were in SO MUCH trouble.

CHAPTER 19

THE BLUES ARE NO JOKE

I was allowed to go to school, the library, and home. Nowhere else.

CeCe and I weren't allowed any TV for the next few weeks, and no desserts.

I didn't know if Nathaniel got into any trouble. Because we weren't speaking.

I didn't want to talk to him.

I sat in the cafeteria at lunch and avoided the school library. He avoided me. It worked out perfectly.

Thanksgiving came and went and was miserable. The only upside was that I was sure Christmas would be worse.

It wasn't fair. It was like for everything we did, there was a shadow version hanging over it. Uncle Ray brought out the tofurkey, but all I saw was the turkey we'd make every year with S-Dad. I helped make butternut squash casserole, but all I saw was the sweet potato casserole S-Dad would let me sprinkle with brown sugar. When we sat down together, I saw a different table, one with S-Dad and Mom holding hands.

It was like *our* house was the haunted house. But I didn't think you could exorcise these ghosts.

Especially because all the while we knew that S-Dad was with a new family, celebrating the holiday together.

How do you deal with something like that?

I didn't know, and none of the adults seemed to either.

In fact, after Thanksgiving dinner, my mom snapped at Auntie Carol, who had been reminding her, again and again, to call her mom, my Poh Poh.

Later, I walked into the kitchen to grab some water. I stopped short at the door when I realized that my mom was sitting at the kitchen table with Uncle Ray, their backs toward me. Her head was in her hands; he had his hand on her shoulder.

"Do you know what it's like to be a woman my age with two failed marriages?" she said, her voice muffled.

"You're young, Lily," Uncle Ray said gently. "You've got a whole life ahead of you."

"Not according to my parents, or the rest of the world for that matter. *He* left, but I'm the one people wonder about. 'What's wrong with her that she's gone through two marriages, two fathers of her kids?' I just can't face them. I just can't talk to my parents right now."

I backed out of the room slowly.

As I'd predicted, Christmas was, in fact, worse.

I hadn't quite realized how hard it would be to keep my face still when the gifts arrived for CeCe, from S-Dad, without even a letter for the rest of us. Then there were email negotiations about CeCe going to California for a visit this summer. Mom didn't want to talk about it, but Uncle Ray told me later that S-Dad didn't want full or even part-time custody of CeCe, just visits. This was the kind of good news that can be reassuring while not actually making you feel better about anything in the slightest.

After Christmas morning gifts, my mom locked herself in her room for the rest of the day and didn't even come out for dinner. Uncle Ray went to try to talk to her, and eventually left a steaming bowl of vegetable pho outside her room. It was still there—cold now, but still fragrant—when I walked by on my way to putting CeCe to bed. I was torn between snatching the bowl up and drinking down the thick, comforting liquid or throwing the bowl against the locked door, smashing it and the lie that food could make everything better, where my mom couldn't miss it.

I chose the first option.

I shared it with CeCe too. She was mostly quiet, and still mad at me, I think. But she drank some, and said thank you.

So I guess that was our holiday moment.

On the last day of break, I sat down with Uncle Ray to listen to a song. It was a song called "Blackbird" by the Beatles.

It was beautiful, simple. It made me want to put my hand on my chest.

And it brought me back to another day, when I thought my heart was going to break apart.

The day after S-Dad left, when I called Laura.

Laura was my *best friend*, the friend I'd known all my life. I knew she'd be there for me.

"Mo, are you okay?!" she'd asked, the moment she picked up the phone.

"No," I said, in a quavering voice. "Something terrible happened. S-Dad . . ." I couldn't find the words to explain how awful everything was. But then, I didn't need to.

"I'm so sorry, Mo," she said. "We're all SO mad at him."

I heard voices in the background, and the sound of Laura moving quickly away, into another room.

"Wait, you know what happened?" I asked. It was impossible—no one knew yet. We'd barely left the house; my mom had barely left her room.

"Well," Laura said awkwardly. "I only found out because, uh . . ."

It hit me.

Our families had known each other for years. Laura's dad and S-Dad were friends. Really good friends.

"Is he THERE?" I demanded. My voice was much higher than I meant it to be, but I couldn't control it.

"Yeah, just last night," Laura said, sounding like she was trying not to cry. "My mom was SO MAD when she heard. He'll only be staying a few more days. I guess he has an apartment being painted . . ." She trailed off desperately. "I'm sorry, Mo!"

I couldn't listen to her, though. He could be talking, be in the background right now, be laughing, happy—happy to have left us. I could hear his voice at any moment.

"I have to go," I said.

"Mo . . . ," Laura said.

"Talk later." Then I hung up the phone with a loud click.

When S-Dad left, we lost our family, and we lost our house. But that wasn't all. We lost our lives in Ridgemont. Everyone on our block, and at my school, knew. Nothing was the same. Neighbors looked at us pityingly whenever we walked by. Teachers asked about my mom in hushed voices. I couldn't bring myself to go to Laura's house anymore. Or even to call, sometimes.

It was as if S-Dad leaving had hit us like an earth-quake, like a fire. And he left a path of destruction that wasn't just about our family. Overnight, everything that had felt good and familiar and safe in Ridgemont was gone.

And now, New Warren felt the same.

I didn't have Laura, I didn't have Nathaniel. I didn't have anyone.

"Whatcha think?" Uncle Ray asked quietly, when the song ended.

"I—I dunno," I said. I shook my head. From the parts I'd heard, the song was all about learning to fly on broken wings. I think it was meant to be hopeful. But that hope felt like such a lie. How would the blackbird fly if its wings were broken? Could it go to the vet? Did the blackbird have health insurance?

"It's okay if it makes you sad," Uncle Ray said. "Great songs do that, sometimes."

"I'm fine," I said softly.

I got up, and went to get ready for school the next day. As I took my things upstairs, I kept my eyes away from the window, and the junkyard. But even not looking at it, I could still *feel* it. Like when you know that eyes are watching you. Like when something is right behind you, reaching but not quite touching you, and all you can do is wait. Like a terrible, empty loneliness.

I faced the first weeks of the New Year with a kind of numb dread. I stuck to my schedule: avoid Nathaniel, sit at an empty table in the cafeteria, repeat the next day.

Weirdly, Peter changed too. It began slowly. It seemed like his friends just didn't find him all that funny anymore. I watched as he went from being at the center of their jokes and conversations, to sitting quietly in their midst, to drifting off on his own. Some lunches, he just went to Ms. Shay's office instead.

It was strange.

I was watching Peter one day, pretending to read, when I was startled by my name.

"Hey, Mo."

I looked up. It was Kerissa.

"We've all been reading Ms. Marvel," she said, nodding toward her table. "You were right, it's INCREDIBLE. We're going to talk about it today. Want to join?"

I smiled. But as nice as it was—I didn't need another friend. Look how that always turned out.

So I shook my head a quiet no. She shrugged.

"Okay. If you change your mind, you know where to find us." And she walked away to join her group.

It had been almost two weeks into the New Year when I came home one day from the library after school, and heard raised voices in the kitchen.

I slipped off my shoes and silently walked in, passing CeCe curled up on the living room couch with her hands pressed over her ears. I gave her shoulder a reassuring squeeze and walked on, toward the kitchen, as the voices became clear.

"Lily, there is nothing wrong with getting help," Uncle Ray said, standing by the sink. "Things can't go on like this, for you or the girls. Just talk to someone."

"Ray, I don't want to hear it," my mom said, her face pale with red spots at her cheeks. "The girls are fine. We're doing fine."

"No, they're not, and neither are you," Uncle Ray said, not quite yelling, but speaking as firmly as I'd ever heard him. "I know this has been hard. But you have to face facts—"

"You are over the line," my mom said, her voice getting louder. "This is *my* family. How dare—"

"Stop yelling at Uncle Ray," I said, the words slipping out before I could stop them.

They both started—neither had noticed me coming in.

"Mo," Uncle Ray said, his voice soothing. "It's fine, we're just talking."

Just as my mom cut in, "Young lady, this is an adult conversation. Don't interrupt."

"Oh, an adult conversation?" I heard myself more than felt myself say it. I tried to tamp the words down into the place where the feelings and upset and anger and sadness stay, but they spilled out. "Like all the other adult things, like taking care of CeCe and packing your kids' lunch and actually spending time with them, that you're so good at doing?"

"Mo," my mom gasped, her face paling like I'd hit her. Uncle Ray made a move as if he couldn't decide which of us to comfort, or stop. But then CeCe came into the kitchen, drawn by my voice, her face wet with tears. Uncle Ray moved decisively then, ushering her out. "C'mon, kiddo," he said kindly, "let's get a movie on for you."

So then it was just me and my mom, alone in the kitchen.

"Mo," my mom said, her voice full of anger and feeling. "How dare you?! I have been working hard to keep this family together, and all you've been doing is getting into trouble and acting out. I need help here."

"Are you KIDDING ME?!" I yelled. My voice was raw and ragged, as all the feelings and words I'd kept down for so long came spilling out. "How dare YOU?!" I asked. "S-Dad isn't the only one who left." I felt my whole body shake as the words spilled out. "S-Dad left us, and so did you! CeCe and I have been all on our own for months now."

"Go, go . . . ," my mom gasped out the words like she couldn't catch a breath.

"What? Go to my closet? We don't even have rooms anymore. And stop pretending like you care or know what's going on. We all know you don't."

I didn't wait for her to respond. I stormed out, making a beeline for the door, grabbing my coat and shoes, not even pausing to put them on.

"Mo, wait!" Uncle Ray called to me from the living room, where he sat with a crying CeCe. But I ignored him. I slammed the door shut behind me, throwing on my shoes and coat as I left. I barely noticed the light dusting of snow on the ground, or felt the cold wind on my face.

She wanted me to help?! She wanted me to do something useful?!

FINE. I would.

I ran, ran like I was being chased, like I was possessed, like my feet had always intended to come back this way.

I ran until I was standing in front of the decaying, uneven front steps of Thomas Childers's house.

I didn't know any rituals; I didn't know any exorcisms.

But still, maybe here I could at least *do* something. I could *solve* something.

I took a deep breath, and in the fading dusk, I put my hand on the rusted doorknob, felt it turn, and plunged inside.

CHAPTER 20

HAUNTINGS

The house smelled of forest, like it was damp, and decaying, but also like things were growing. Tree branches had wormed their way inside. I could see holes where animals had chewed through. There was snow inside too, from broken windows and cracks in the ones that were boarded up.

In the early evening light, I could make out where the walls were peeling away like putty, and caught glimpses of the rotting boards behind them. There were piles of debris everywhere—wood, pieces of the wall, pieces of the ceiling, ivy, stones, dirt. It was a different world, like inside and outside had all gotten mixed up.

There wasn't much furniture. From the hall, I could see there was an old table in one of the front rooms. And in another . . .

I blinked and tried to get closer.

Walking across the old floor made my heart pound. I had to skirt some holes that led, I guessed, to some kind of basement below that I did NOT want to know more about.

But I made it, walking unsteadily around beams and grit.

It was a desk, in the corner of what I'm guessing must have been a study. It was mildewed and gave off a musty, rotten smell. But I could tell it had once been big and grand. And across the top, in deep, cursive letters, someone had engraved: Childers.

I reached for one of the drawers and pulled it open. There was dust and dirt inside, and what I'd guess were the crumbling remains of papers.

Had Thomas Childers sat at this desk?

Is this where he'd dreamed up his circus, made his plans?

Had he known then all the terrible things he'd do to make them come true?

Is this where his father sat as he read his letter?

I turned away and kept walking. There was another room in the back that I think was the kitchen. In the dark, I could make out what looked like a big rusty tub, and some larger shapes that I could only just see the outlines of in the darkness. Part of me wanted to go see what they were, but the floor was even worse in this room—all torn up, with old nails and bits of wood and jagged edges sticking up every which way.

And suddenly, I wasn't in the old Childers house anymore. I was staring at those jagged, sharp edges of the floor, and instead of seeing them, I saw another kitchen.

See, after S-Dad left, right after New Year's, my mom was so sad. But she was also strong. Strong, I realize now, for us. She made things into a game.

When we had to box up S-Dad's things, she said that the person who boxed fastest would get to pick the pizza toppings for dinner.

At the end of one very bad week, when we were all sad, she took me and CeCe out of school for a special family day. We bundled up in our warmest clothes, drove to the ocean, and walked around with ice cream, daring the cold to do its worst, feeling invincible.

She told us we could talk to her about anything. She asked how we were doing. When people asked how she was, she answered honestly, head high.

And watching her, I knew that we were going to be okay.

Even though the weeks and months that followed were hard, even though things with Laura were strange and different, even though our house felt empty and every corner held memories that would jump out without warning, even though my mom would look at bills with a pinch between her eyes, I knew we would get through this.

Until one day, in April, when everything changed.

CeCe had been with S-Dad on a weekend visit.

"Mo, guess what?" she said, running into the kitchen when she got home. "I'm going to be a big sister!"

It took a minute for the words to make sense.

And then they did.

I saw my mom behind CeCe, hearing what she'd said.

And I saw her face crumple.

A few nights later, I woke up to a strange noise.

I went into the kitchen. There was my mom, in her pajamas, tearing up the old plastic floorboards. With her hands.

"It's no use," she said, not looking up. "I've been trying, but we can't afford this house on my salary. We have to sell it, and he wants half. Says he needs it for the new..." She swallowed the words that followed. "And who knows how much we'll have to spend to get someone to buy it, we'll need to fix the porch, not to mention the cost of the fire repairs..." She trailed off. But I felt her words land like a cut deep in my chest. She ripped up another piece of flooring with an awful sucking, tearing sound. "We're going to lay down fake tiling, that will make the kitchen look nicer." She tore again, in a way you are *definitely* not supposed to, leaving jagged and sharp edges.

"Mom, we can do this tomorrow," I said. "In daylight. With tools. I can help."

"Just let me be, I've got it," she said.

Her hands were bleeding, nicked by the sharp edges of the tiling.

"Seriously, Mo, just go," she said. "I've got it."

I stayed and helped, of course.

I mean, you can't just leave your mom like that.

After that, things were different. Learning about S-Dad's new family was like the final snow that starts an avalanche slicing down. I watched my mom get quieter and sadder. She folded in on herself until only a stretched-out shadow was left. She didn't feel like my mom anymore. And then she lost her job. And then we drifted here.

Since then, I've never wanted to leave her without someone to watch her. That was when I realized that I had to step up. I had to take care of her, and of CeCe.

So that's what I did.

And that's what I do.

I've been wondering, lately, if this is how Maudie felt too.

What was her life like? Was she one day happy with her family and then the next day, *poof*—all gone? How did she feel when her life was suddenly all the circus, all about someone else and what he wanted? How did she feel when she was left to deal with all the jagged pieces?

I used to think fear was something that jumped out at you in the dark. But some fear is different. Some fear pools in your skin and lives in your bones.

And how do you deal with that kind of fear, the kind that's so much a part of you that you can't tell where it ends and you begin?

How do you exorcise that?

A sound brought me back to where I was: to the old, forgotten, awful house.

Creeak.

I spun around. It was coming from upstairs.

I peered up the stairwell, which was rotting, with steps caving in on themselves.

Was something up there? Was there anything here?

As if in answer, all of a sudden, I heard another loud *creeeeaaak.*

I wanted to bolt then and there. But instead, inexplicably I took a step *forward.*

"Why can't you leave us alone?" I called into the dark. "Why can't you leave her alone? Let Maudie go!"

My voice echoed through the empty house. My feet left prints in the layers of muck and dust.

Creeeak. The noise was all around me. Like the house was taking a breath. Like something in it was alive. And it knew I was there.

"Answer me!" I yelled. "That's the least you could do!"

All at once, it felt like night set in, like when you're watching the moment when the sun slips below the horizon, and in an instant, everything is two shades darker.

The door felt miles away. I was here, alone, exposed.

"Leave us alone!" I yelled again at the surrounding dark.

Creeeeak, went the house. But closer, this time.

And then I knew that there was something creeping toward me, something dark and hungry, something that didn't care about me or Maudie or anyone else but itself.

I panicked and stumbled back toward the door. But my foot caught on one of the fallen beams, and I went flying, landing at the base of the writing desk. I was aware, from somewhere far away, that my ankle hurt.

Creeeak.

It was reaching for me, like the dark was stretching out, like it wanted to pull me deeper into the house.

It had hurt Maudie, and now it wanted to hurt me. *Again.*

And suddenly, I was OVER it.

I pulled the leg that didn't hurt back and KICKED. *BAM.*

My foot hit the writing desk, Thomas Childers's desk, his father's desk, all their desks stretching back through the generations.

BAM. I hit it again, so hard it crunched against the wall.

BAM. One of the legs went askew and the desk tipped to the side. I leveraged myself closer so I could kick and kick and kick.

"Leave her alone!" I screamed. "Leave us alone! Go away! I HATE YOU!"

I kicked and kicked, and dust and dirt and gravel swirled up from the floor, like the house was responding, like it wasn't used to anyone fighting back.

And then—

BAM.

The door flew open.

"MO!"

Nathaniel was there, pulling me to my feet.

I looked back. The desk was a pile of wood and splinters.

"Come on, Mo," Nathaniel said.

I put my arm around his shoulder, and leaning into each other, we made our escape into the welcome cold of the night.

"How did you find me?" I asked, as we hobbled outside.

"Uncle Ray called. He said you'd run away. I had a feeling you'd be here."

I blinked, almost dazed that the outside world still existed. It was dark outside. How long had I been in there?

We limped down the path, and Nathaniel's face was determined and grim. I wanted to say something, but what could I say, after how awful I'd been to him?

Besides, it was taking all my concentration to put one foot in front of the other.

So we walked in silence.

Uncle Ray had the door open by the time we reached the yard, and he and my mom ran out, both talking at once. Uncle Ray helped me inside, and as he did, I turned back to look at Nathaniel. But he was already on his bike and pedaling away.

Inside, CeCe clung to me, and Uncle Ray inspected my foot and declared it "just a sprain."

Once she was sure I was okay, my mom went back to her room, and didn't come out at all that night.

But it was kind of a relief. I didn't know what I'd say if she did want to talk to me.

Uncle Ray said I didn't need to go to school the next day, to rest my foot. He helped me upstairs, and I got into bed.

I didn't want to sleep, though.

What would happen? What would I dream?

Would Childers come and get revenge?

Would Maudie come to me, looking disappointed, like she needed help that I wasn't giving?

But I must have been tired.

Because I fell asleep so quickly, I barely had time to worry.

And I don't know if it was a good sign, or a bad sign, that when I closed my eyes and slept, there was nothing but total, quiet darkness.

CHAPTER 21

GRILLED CHEESE MAKES (SOME) THINGS BETTER

The next morning, I stayed in bed until Mom left for work. I planned to stay there all day, and possibly for the next calendar year. Except around eleven, Uncle Ray knocked.

"Lunch is tomato soup and grilled cheese, and you only get some if you come downstairs," he called.

Which is nefarious.

We ate in silence. Uncle Ray fed scraps of cheese to Serenity, and for a while, there was just the sound of spoons in bowls.

"Music?" I asked, just as we were both finishing.

"Mmm, in a sec," he said. I almost choked on my last spoonful of soup. Uncle Ray *never* says no to music.

He put his hands on the table and cleared his throat like he was about to call a meeting to order.

"Here's the thing, in our family. We don't talk," he said.

"Huh?" I said.

"That's how I was raised," he explained. "Same with my big brother, your Gung Gung, and then that's how he raised your mom. There's no talking about feelings. If you have a bad moment, or a fight, or anything, you just move on. Don't mention it again."

I didn't really see where he was going with this, and I think he saw it on my face.

"That's why music is my thing. It says what you don't know how to put into words."

"Oh." Now *that* made sense. "Is that why you worked in music?" I asked.

"Yup. When I found music, it was the first time I found my people. The ones who understood me, you know?"

"I do," I said. I thought for a beat. "What did your mom and dad say? About your job?" I'd never thought to ask about my great-grandparents before. I know they were very traditional, but that was all, really.

"Nothing," Uncle Ray said. "They would have flipped if they knew I was dropping out of school to go into music. So I told them I was in electronics, and they just never asked. That's how we got by."

"Wow," said. "So it worked out, but . . ."

Uncle Ray nodded vigorously.

"Exactly. It's sad, right? And now, I wish I'd told them. Broken the cycle. It would have been hard. But

I think it might have opened a door between us. Maybe we could have changed."

"But," I sighed, "how do you know that the change will actually happen? How are you so sure that what comes next is good, and not, I dunno, just more of the awful stuff?"

"You just have to choose," Uncle Ray said. "You choose to believe that things can be better. Look at music."

I didn't quite see the connection.

"Rock, R and B, music in general." Uncle Ray spread his arms wide. "It's about new ways of being, not having to follow the patterns and rules of the past."

"Is . . ." I thought back to the songs we had listened to, and the one I kept coming back to. "Is that what 'dancing in the dark' means? Not knowing what's out there, but just . . . dancing forward anyway?"

"Could be," he said.

I felt like we'd started talking about music, and now we were talking about a lot of other things.

"Music?" Uncle Ray asked, after a long pause.

"Yes," I said. "But before we do. Can I ask you something kind of personal?"

"Go for it."

"Are you . . . happy?" I said finally. "Being alone? I mean, not being married or anything? Because Mom's not happy."

"I am," he said. "I'm very happy."

"But you're by yourself."

"Yeah, but that's because I want to be. I've had girl-friends, and I've had boyfriends. But right now, I'm just happy being me. Happiness and sadness come for us all, you know, whether we're alone, or with other people."

"Oh," I said, taking it all in. "Okay."

We went to the music room and sat down in our chairs.

Uncle Ray pressed play.

We spent the rest of the afternoon listening to music. Uncle Ray played me "Angel" by Jimi Hendrix, and "At Last" by Etta James, and so many more.

Some of the songs were happy, some were sad. And some were an emotion that I can't describe. They echoed like a feeling that lives in your bones and doesn't need labels.

The music played, and I let it carry me along.

CHAPTER 22

A DREAM, A PROMISE

That night, I closed my eyes in my bed and opened them in the old Childers house.

It was another dream; I knew that right away.

And I wasn't alone.

Next to me was the white dog—Maudie. She was lit from inside, like a star.

"You shouldn't have to be here," I said. "He shouldn't get to control you."

There was noise then, from outside. The door burst open.

It was Nathaniel, Nathaniel wearing the same jacket he had on when he'd found me that night. His face was terrified but determined. For me.

He raced into the house, and then disappeared, like the memory had exhausted itself. But I'd seen what was important.

Nathaniel had been scared, but he was there for me anyway.

And doing something—acting—made him brave.

I looked around the house. It was the same house

that had so terrified me before, with its dark corners and shadows and ripped-up floors.

Was I still scared? Yes.

But it wasn't the chest-clenching, stomach-tightening terror of before.

I looked around.

It was just a place.

I turned back to Maudie to find that she'd changed. She was Maudie the elephant now, but not towering as I'd seen her before. Instead, her belly scraped the floor. Her feet were sunk into the jagged floorboard. She was trapped.

"I've been all wrong," I said. "Haven't I?"

She looked at me solemnly.

"I thought I had to do something about Childers. But I can't change him, or reach him."

Almost shyly, I held my hand out to her.

"But I *can* help you. Like Nathaniel helped me. I *will* help you."

She reached back, draping her trunk around my shoulders in a firm, warm embrace.

I put my forehead against hers, feeling her cool, wrinkled skin against mine.

"You aren't alone," I said. "Neither of us has to be alone."

Then, as everything began to go fuzzy, a quiet voice whispered through the night.

"Don't go," CeCe's faraway voice echoed around me. "Don't leave me, Mo."

"I promise," I whispered back.

When I woke up, I was in my bed, only with my feet on my pillow, and my head at the end of the bed, and a blanket over my top half.

I got up and tiptoed into the room, careful not to wake CeCe. I looked out the window, into the junkyard, for a long time.

I knew what I had to do.

CHAPTER 23

FRIENDS?

Walking into the library the next day felt almost as scary as walking into the old Childers house.

Nathaniel was at our usual table. His head was down as he stared quietly at his sandwich. He didn't see me until I stopped at the table.

Nathaniel's head whirled up, surprise and dread on his face.

"Mo . . . ," he said hesitantly.

"Wait please," I said, feeling my stomach twist, and hoping he didn't hate me too much. "I know you probably don't want to speak to me again. And I understand," I continued, talking fast so he couldn't walk away before I'd finished. "But, I just want you to know that I'm sorry. I shouldn't have said what I did. Any of it. It was awful, and unforgivable, and I didn't mean it, and never should have said it. And I'm just . . . sorry. Just really, really sorry."

The silence felt like it stretched out for forever. I stared at the table, scared to look up. Maybe he'd never forgive me. Maybe I should just leave . . .

Nathaniel's chair pushed back with a screech, and he enveloped me in a hug.

"I'M sorry, Mo!" he said, squeezing me tightly. "I was IRRESPONSIBLE and mean and I thought you'd hate me forever."

I was so relieved I thought I'd fall over. But I didn't. Instead, I hugged Nathaniel back.

We sat down at our table, in our usual spots. Nathaniel opened his mouth to talk, but I plunged on. I knew what I needed to say, and I knew that if I stopped, I might lose courage.

"I never told you why we moved."

"Yeah, but you don't have to if you don't want to," he said.

"I know," I said. "But the thing is, I kind of do want to tell you, if that's okay, of course."

"Of course," he said.

So I told him about S-Dad. And the day he left. And fires, and toast. And my mom and the kitchen floor, and all the days of worries in between and ever since. I told him about how I hadn't spoken to Laura in months, and couldn't bring myself to answer the phone when she called.

And I told him other things too. Things I hadn't thought about in a while. Like how my mom told me that S-Dad had a hard life when he was a kid, how his dad was not nice to him, and not a good guy. Which makes things extra jumbled. Because can you hate someone you also feel a little sad for? Could this be why S-Dad did what he did?

"Well, that's awful," Nathaniel said when I trailed off, "but I also don't think it's an excuse. I mean, your stepdad is an adult. He could have chosen different, you know? And I'm really, really sorry that all of this happened, I mean I can't imagine . . ." Nathaniel floundered for words, but I knew what he meant.

After a minute, Nathaniel took a deep breath and squared his shoulders.

"And I'm really, REALLY sorry. I should have told you about Peter. We've been friends since kindergarten. Then his parents divorced, and it was really messy, and they were arguing about where Peter should live. And Peter just changed. He was SO mean. And the worst part is . . ." Nathaniel looked at the table, his cheeks going red. "I was mean too. That's why I come here during lunch. I don't think anyone really wants to hang out with me. And I knew it was wrong, but I'd laugh at Peter's jokes and make fun of people just like he did. I," he faltered. "I feel awful about it. And then when I realized I couldn't do it anymore, I should have tried to talk to him. I should have explained, or tried to get him to stop. But instead I just disappeared."

We sat in silence for a minute.

I understood. I mean, I was literally avoiding the phone every time it rang, in case it was Laura. I had been alone; I had made myself alone, just like Nathaniel.

And it had been such a relief to have Nathaniel on my side.

Then I remembered my dream. And Maudie. Who was still alone.

I was ready to stop avoiding things. I was ready to face them head-on.

"I have a plan," I blurted out. "For Maudie. She still needs our help. I mean, if you still want to help. I understand if you don't . . ."

"Another ghost plan?" Nathaniel said. "What is it?"

I took a breath, getting my thoughts in order.

"I think we've been wrong. I think we've been too focused on Childers, and worrying about him. Why should he have all this power over Maudie? Why should *he* control what happens to her?" I was getting heated and a little loud, but I didn't care just then.

"It isn't right," I said. "And it's not fair. So I say, forget him. Let's ignore him. Let's bring Maudie peace. It's the idea you've had from the very beginning. We know where she's buried—in the junkyard. We'll have a ceremony there, to help her move on. And I know when. We'll have it on the anniversary of the fire, in March.

We'll have the ceremony, and we'll help Maudie once and for all."

"Aren't you worried about Childers?" Nathaniel asked. "I mean, what about your yard?"

"He's the one who should be worried about me," I said grimly. "And besides, we'll come prepared. I have New Warren's number one ghost expert, after all."

Nathaniel smiled.

"I'm in," he said.

"So . . ." I took a deep breath. "Friends?"

"Friends," he said.

CHAPTER 24

A STEADY RHYTHM . . . UNTIL IT'S NOT

Over the next few weeks, our lives fell into a rhythm. And weirdly, things began to feel almost . . . normal.

I spent most afternoons with Nathaniel except the days he had Hebrew school. After school, we'd either go to my house to listen to music with Uncle Ray, or we'd go to the library, do homework, and talk with Lavender.

I even had dinner at Nathaniel's house and got to meet all his siblings. They were really nice and VERY outgoing. They all clearly loved Nathaniel, though I could also understand why it might be a bit hard being the youngest, ghost-obsessed, quieter brother.

At school, things were changing too.

Now, during study hall, Nathaniel would walk me to Ms. Shay's office before heading to the library.

And actually, talking with Ms. Shay was really, really helping.

She said it was okay to be mad.

She said to notice when I was mad.

And even though the feelings still simmered, and still hurt, I felt like I could live with them. Like they were important, somehow.

So things were NOT perfect, and I was still mad at my mom.

But life felt a little easier.

Maybe that's why, one day, when I was walking to the library for lunch, I did something I'd never done before.

I saw Kerissa walking toward the cafeteria.

"Hey!" I called out, before I could talk myself out of it. "Did everyone like the book?"

"Of course." She grinned, her freckles rippling like a happy wave across her face. "Kamala Khan is the best!"

"Right?!" I said. I saw Nathaniel out of the corner of my eye and waved him over.

"You know Nathaniel, right?"

"Oh hey, of course! I haven't seen you much," she said.

"Uh, I've been eating lunch in the library," Nathaniel said awkwardly.

"Well, want to join us?" she asked, looking between us.

"Really?!" Nathaniel said, with a giant smile.

"We'd love to," I said.

So suddenly, I found myself walking through that crowded, scary cafeteria again. Only this time with Nathaniel next to me and a table of people to join. And before I knew it, we were talking about books and comics, and it was really nice and not scary at all.

Impressive, right?

As if all this wasn't enough, Peter wasn't bothering us anymore. I thought he'd be after us more than ever, after that night at the Childers house. But now, he barely spoke to me, or anyone else it seemed. He was quiet, and spent most of his time alone. It was strange. But, it made our lives easier. I decided not to worry about it.

Of course, not everything had fallen into place. Sometimes, when I left for school, CeCe made me promise that I'd come back. I guess I'd really scared her that night I ran out, and I didn't know how to fix it.

Instead, I focused on preparing for March, for when we'd set Maudie free. Things were quiet in the junkyard, and in Uncle Ray's yard too. I wondered if maybe whatever I'd met in Childers's house had gone back to sleep.

I remembered my dream.

The junkyard was just a place, Thomas Childers was just the memory of a person.

This can work, I told myself. *There's nothing to be scared of.*

Which shows you just how much I know.

CHAPTER 25

BACK TO THE JUNKYARD

On the last Saturday in March, I was wide awake when the sun rose.

Today was the day. The anniversary of the fire. Today, we'd finally lay Maudie the elephant to rest.

I looked over my checklist for the thousandth time.

I had Maudie's blue marble. Then, following Nathaniel's example, I'd scoured Uncle Ray's house for anything I could find that might help.

For example, my mom had once told me that her parents used to light incense for Chinese ceremonies. So, when I found some in Uncle Ray's cabinet, I asked if I could use it. (Uncle Ray said yes, which was great. But Nathaniel was bringing the matches—I couldn't quite face that on my own.)

I also had a Buddha figurine from Uncle Ray's study, a giant bag of salt from the kitchen, and a red sweater to wear (it's a lucky color on Lunar New Year, so why not now?).

And finally, after a lot of debate, we'd decided to bring Childers's top hat along too. We would leave it behind, in the junkyard, where it belonged.

But despite all these plans, on the morning of the ceremony, I realized I wanted one more thing.

I was putting my shoes on when Serenity came up behind me and yipped.

"Relax, Serenity," I said, knowing that Serenity never relaxes.

He yipped again, looking at me, and then the door.

"Aw, he wants to go with you," Uncle Ray said. "Want to take him on your walk?"

"Uhhhh . . . ," I said. I looked at Serenity, who glared at me, but then yipped again.

"Sure."

So that's how I walked Serenity into the center of town, to the candy store, to buy some salted peanuts. I wanted Maudie to have something nice to remember me by.

We were almost there when I looked up and saw a familiar face.

It was Unofficial Tour Guide.

"Hello, hello!" He waved as we made eye contact, jogging to close the space between us on the sidewalk. Serenity narrowed his eyes and let out a warning rumble.

I can't lie: I was flattered that Serenity was growling at someone other than me.

"Er." Unofficial Tour Guide took a step back. "Can I interest you in some material about New Warren?" he asked, trying to ignore my murderous Chihuahua. "We have some wonderful history here, and great visitor locations."

"I'm from here," I snapped. I meant to just brush by and walk on, but he blinked at me with that owlish look. And suddenly, I realized that I'd seen his photo— one where he was much younger, with brown hair, and no glasses yet, but that same wide-eyed expression.

"WAIT," I said, stopping suddenly. "You wrote the book on the founding families of New Warren! The one with the section on the Childers family!"

That's why the author photo had seemed familiar.

"You read my book?!" he exclaimed. "What did you think?!"

"Uh, it was interesting," I said, not wanting to lie.

He gave me a startlingly perceptive look.

"Be honest," he said. "I never say no to feedback."

"Well," I said, trying to think of a way to say it without being mean. "Okay. I think it's great that you love history. But I think maybe you don't see the full story."

"How so?" he asked with a frown.

"Well . . . for example, you give Thomas Childers a lot of credit, but you don't think about the other people in the story. What about the Indigenous people the Childers family and all the town founders stole their land from? What happened to them? What about the people he used, and displayed in his circus, and didn't pay well to get where he was? Did his family own slaves? What were their lives like? If you like history, then you have to commit to thinking about everyone in it as a person. That's what Lavender says. She's a librarian," I added, just in case he didn't know.

"You . . . ," he said, a line right in between his eyes. "You . . . make a convincing argument."

"I do?" I asked, startled. I'd sort of expected him to argue or get mad.

"You've given me a lot to think about," he said. "Thank you."

"Oh. Uh, you're welcome," I said awkwardly.

I knew I should just walk away while I was ahead, but something about the way he'd listened made me go on.

"Also," I said, not in a mad way, just stating a fact, "I'm from here."

"Hmm?" he asked.

"New Warren. I'm from here. It shouldn't be that surprising."

"You're right," he said. "Well, young lady, I feel suitably chastened. I will reflect on what you've said, I promise you. But also, in the meantime, if you're still interested in the Childers family, and the other people around them, perhaps you should talk to the descendants."

"Descendants?" I asked.

"Yes, the direct descendants still live here. They have a different last name now, which I can't remember." His brow wrinkled. "But they still own the old house. Shame how they've let it fall apart." He shook his head mournfully. "They wouldn't talk to me for the book, but perhaps they'll chat with you. I believe the son is in the local middle school—you might know him. He's named for Thomas P. Childers."

"Hmm," I said. "I haven't met a Thomas, but I can ask."

"Maybe he already graduated. Huh, my memory's not what it used to be . . . Well, I'll think on what you said, young lady. I'm not as stuck in my ways as all that."

I waved goodbye and kept going, and didn't say what I was really feeling. Which was that even if he was in my class, I wasn't super interested in meeting *anyone* from the Childers family. And that soon, I wouldn't have to worry about the Childerses ever again.

I got peanuts, and then went to meet Nathaniel at his house.

"Mo, WHAT IS HAPPENING?" Nathaniel asked,

coming down from the porch, eyes wide as he looked at Serenity.

"He wanted to come with me. Can you believe it?!" I reached down to pet Serenity. He allowed me one pat before he growled. So, progress.

We were walking down the road, back to Uncle Ray's, when two police cars zoomed by, sirens blaring.

"Huh," Nathaniel said. It was kind of unusual for New Warren.

We stopped at home so I could drop Serenity off and get my bag for the ceremony. Serenity gave me one small bump with his nose in what I think was a "Thank you," growled at Nathaniel, and then raced off to find Uncle Ray in his music room. My mom was in her room, so if I could just get my bag, we could make it out without any questions—

"Where are you going?" CeCe asked, arms crossed. She sat on the living room couch, glaring at me.

"We're just hanging out," I said. "I'll be back in two hours, tops."

She looked at me suspiciously.

I sighed. I went to turn on the TV.

"Here!" I said. "Why don't you watch something? I'm sure Mom won't mind."

I found one of her favorite shows, which seemed to work.

We hurried into the yard. I checked the windows

to make sure no one was watching, and then Nathaniel was up the tree, and over the junkyard fence. As I climbed to follow him, I saw the living room curtain move. But when I looked closer, there was nothing there. Hopefully, CeCe hadn't seen us.

I took a deep breath and followed Nathaniel over the fence, into the junkyard.

In the daylight, the junkyard was yet another new landscape. The piles of junk and dirt didn't look scary so much as startling. Old lampposts and bedsprings seemed fused together, like they'd been left here so long that they'd morphed into new creatures and landmarks.

We moved faster in the light, and in no time, we were back at the spot where we'd found Childers's hat—with the blankets and piles and bits of caution tape.

I drew out the incense stick and set my bag down by a metal sheet.

"Okay," I said quietly. "I think we should start with incense. To cleanse the area."

Nathaniel nodded and took out his lighter.

I almost managed to hold my hands still as he lit the incense. The stick smoked, not burned, which helped.

I held it out solemnly, aware of what a serious

moment this was. I barely even reacted when I realized that the incense was . . . berry scented?

I waved it around anyway—hoping ghosts didn't mind that sort of thing.

"Okay," I said, after I'd waved it in every direction, and all around Childers's hat for good measure. "Now, let's get the chalk out, and—"

I paused as a siren screamed close by, and another police car came racing down the road, and then past the junkyard.

"I hope everything's okay," Nathaniel said.

"Yeah," I agreed. "Okay," I said, turning back to my bag. "So next, we're going to get chalk, and then we'll identify the spot where we think Maudie was most likely laid to rest—"

"What is that SMELL?" a voice said, cutting me off.

I spun around, and Nathaniel dropped the lighter in surprise.

It was like a distorted version of the night at the Childers house.

There, like he'd appeared out of nowhere, was Peter.

But he looked different. Peter had reddened, wild eyes, and looked stranger and scarier than I'd ever seen him.

"Oh," he said, looking toward the top hat that lay on the ground. "So *you're* the one that took the hat. Do you know how much trouble I got in when I lost it? It had just been sitting on a dusty shelf in our house, but still, it was all my fault when I borrowed it and it went missing."

And that's when it all came together.

Uncle Ray's mailbox could have been destroyed by an iron hook.

But it also could have been a baseball bat.

The fire in the junkyard had broken out right by the hidden shelter. The shelter that was too small for an adult to stand in comfortably, but fine for a middle schooler.

"Maybe this *is* my business," Peter had said, on the crumbling porch of the Childers house. "Maybe you're trespassing."

"I have weird dreams sometimes," Peter had said.

Nathaniel said spirits could attach to a house or a place. Or a *person*.

"It's you," I said. "Thomas P. Childers. The P is for Peter. You're his descendant."

I heard Nathaniel's surprised intake of breath from beside me.

Peter smiled, a joyless, hollow-eyed smile.

Then he bent down and picked up Nathaniel's lighter.

Click, click, went the lighter.

And holding it up, he came toward us.

CHAPTER 26

SPRING STORMS

"H-have you been here all night?" Nathaniel asked haltingly.

I couldn't speak, or move even. I was rooted to the spot, watching Peter play with the lighter in his hand.

Peter shrugged.

"What do you care?" he asked, his voice strange and angry.

Click, click, went the lighter.

Another siren wailed and we heard, rather than saw, another car speed past us.

"Are they looking for you, Pete?" Nathaniel asked.

"I'm not going back there," Peter said fiercely in reply. He took a step forward. "You better not tell anyone or I'll, I'll . . ."

I held out the incense stick like it could keep him away.

But he trailed off, not finishing the sentence.

Instead he just slumped, blinking at us. Like he was exhausted. Like he didn't know what to do either.

Peter looked at the lighter in his hand.

"I have the weirdest dreams sometimes," he said. "About this place."

Click, click, went the lighter.

If you'd told me I was going to meet the person possibly controlled by the ghost of Thomas Childers, I would have imagined him with glowing eyes, or a ghostly figure beside him.

But Peter just looked small. And sad.

And standing here, where I'd dreamed of Maudie so many times, it hit me. Maudie came to me in my dreams. Maybe it was the same for Peter. And to dream of Thomas Childers? That must have been really . . . scary.

"We can figure this out," Nathaniel was saying.

"Oh, what do you know, Saint Nathaniel?" Peter snapped. "Why do you care anyway? You don't want anything to do with me, right, Mo? I'm a bad person."

I looked at Peter, really looked. His eyes were red from crying.

I didn't see the boy who'd been mean to me; I didn't even see the last descendant of Thomas Childers.

I didn't think when I responded.

"You're not a bad person," I said. I took a step toward him. "You're just not. You're hurt and scared and maybe mean sometimes. But that doesn't mean you're bad."

I held out my hand to him, like Maudie had done all those times, in my dreams, to me.

"I don't think you have to go through this alone," I said.

Peter looked at my outstretched hand, dazed.

But before he could speak, a howl cut through the junkyard, and the wind whipped around us.

Like we were waking from a trance, we all looked up, all became aware that it was darker than it had been a few minutes ago, that thick clouds had descended across the sun.

The wind wailed and it blew again, so strong that I stumbled forward.

And then I felt it. The same feeling I'd had in Thomas Childers's house, that dark, heavy force that made my lungs constrict and the hairs on the back of my neck stand on end.

"Mo?" Nathaniel called out to me, yelling to be heard over the wind.

"What's going on?!" Peter cried, eyes wide in fear.

"It's Childers!" I shouted. "He's here!"

"A . . . a ghost?!" Peter was pale and scared and looking to *me* for help, like I could do something.

The wind howled and screamed, and leaves whipped at my face.

Peter took my hand.

Peter reached out to Nathaniel and they gripped hands tightly as we turned to face the growing dark.

"The ritual, Nathaniel!" I said, yelling over the storm. "We have to do the exorcism! For Childers!"

"I—I don't remember it," Nathaniel said, his breath coming out in gasps, his chest heaving. "I don't remember any of them!"

I could practically feel his fear as he gasped out a few words, some I think in Latin, some I think in Hebrew, some I think that were just panicked sounds. They were all clearly running together in his head. And I couldn't blame him.

The wind hit the ground like a hand smacking the dirt. Bits of dust and rocks flew up in the air. I covered my eyes as something sharp whipped toward my face. Nathaniel and Peter ducked as a batter of small sticks flew over their heads. I wasn't fast enough, and something nicked my cheek, though I barely had time to feel the sting. Rain lashed down, and thunder rumbled, and the wind blew hard as if to separate us. The incense extinguished in my hand, and then flew out of reach.

What were we going to do?

And suddenly, in the dark, something else seemed to loom. In the whistling and whirling leaves and debris, it was almost like I could see a figure, an outline I knew

211

from the bust in the library, and the photographs I'd seen on display.

And then, before my eyes, it changed. Thomas Childers's profile morphed into something more familiar, sprouting curly hair and extending into a tall, thin silhouette.

S-Dad.

Peter also gasped.

"Dad?" he said.

For a moment, I was confused. S-Dad didn't look anything like Peter's dad.

"No, that's not true!" Peter said, like the shadow was talking to him. "Mo, it's not him, is it?" he asked frantically.

Then I understood, though I didn't know how to say it. We were all seeing something different in the shadows.

"I didn't mean it," Nathaniel's voice was cracking, as he looked at the shadow with big, desperate eyes. "Please, Zayde, you have to believe me. I'll make you proud, I *will*, I *can*—"

"Is it really my dad?" Peter asked, his voice high with fear.

"No," I got out. "And yes."

The shadow loomed; it seemed to grow, and expand, and slither toward us all at once.

S-Dad was closer now. I could see his eyes, his disappointment.

"You made your feelings clear, Mo," he said. "How could I love someone like you?"

The shadow peaked like a wave about to engulf us.

"You're the real danger, Mo," S-Dad said. "Look what you did to our family."

There was no air left in my chest. I wanted to break into tiny pieces, to disappear.

But then Peter gripped my hand even tighter.

He turned to me, his voice a whisper full of pain, but also, something like . . . strength.

"I don't want to be like him," Peter said, his voice low and true, rain and tears intermingling on his face. "I won't be like him," he said. "He can't make me. Can he?"

"No," I said, trying to convince myself as much as Peter. "What he's saying isn't true," I said, voice louder, trying to reach Nathaniel, even as I was aware that the dark was growing, surrounding us.

"It's a trick. He can't make us—"

I gasped, as it hit me like a rush of sound. "THAT'S IT," I said.

I turned to Peter, to Nathaniel. Absurdly, I *smiled*.

"We're dancing in the dark!" I said.

"Um, WHAT?!" Nathaniel's voice high with fear,

Peter was wide-eyed with confusion. "Mo, now is NOT the time for music," Nathaniel screeched.

"No," I shouted over the wind. "That's the *answer*." I looked out to the dark, closing in on us. "Everything is dark and terrible, but we're still here," I said to it, to the two boys beside me. "We're making something new. We get to *choose*."

The wind picked up, and Nathaniel and Peter moved in closer, like if we were separated we'd be blown away. The shadow, the shape, closed in.

"Mo, what are you talking about?!" Nathaniel cried desperately.

But it was the strangest thing. I knew what to do.

Nathaniel had said that even though there were all these rituals and rules and ceremonies, all we really needed for the ritual was willpower. At its core, that's what it was about. And I knew that we had it.

"Hey!" I called into the shadows. "You think you're scary? Well, you're nothing but a small, mean memory."

The wind howled in response.

"You're just hurting other people because you can't handle that you messed up!" I called. "I'm sorry about your dad. But you can't hurt other people. And you WON'T. Because it wasn't Maudie's fault," I yelled out. "It wasn't my mom's fault! And it wasn't my fault either!"

And as I screamed it into the wind, I knew it was as clear and true as the purest note of music.

I felt Nathaniel and Peter straighten to face the wind beside me.

"It wasn't my fault!" I yelled into the wind again.

"You can't control me," Peter shouted. "I don't have to be like you!"

"You can't change me," Nathaniel yelled, the loudest I'd ever heard him. "My Zayde loved me just the way I am, and he knew I loved him too!"

"Thomas Childers, we're still here!" I yelled.

"We get to be ourselves!" Nathaniel called.

"We get to mess up!" Peter yelled. "We get to change!"

The darkness reared up, and I felt its anger, a life compounded by cycles and cycles of hate and bitterness.

But I wasn't scared.

Our shouts and the wind and the rain merged into a chorus of sound, a song pulsing with everything in it: rage and sadness and joy and life.

I looked up, staring into the black of the storm.

"We're so much more than you," I said.

My voice was quiet now, but it rang through the wind like a note cutting through a packed stadium, reaching out in a way that no words can. Its truth reverberated and echoed through the quietest places inside me, places where music began and resounded, places that were the opposite of fear.

The wind howled once more, but this time like a wail, like a goodbye.

Like something was banished; like something was free.

And just like that, it was over.

CHAPTER 27

SAFE

I was curled up on the chair in Uncle Ray's music room, with Serenity at my feet. CeCe sat on the floor, drawing, and my mom was doing a crossword in the easy chair. Uncle Ray had put on an album, and calm, easy music unfurled through the room.

It might sound like a dream (I mean, SERENITY was at my feet?).

But it wasn't.

I reached up to touch the cut on my cheek, as if to double-check that I was awake. It was already healing, just a day after the storm.

I sat there and thought about what had happened in the junkyard.

I didn't know if I could put it into words. How one moment there had been noise everywhere, and the next: silence.

How could I describe that moment when the wind stopped, and the leaves fell to the ground with a wet sigh?

When after the storm, there was silence, but a

silence that was full somehow? All around us the air had hummed with a simple, quiet aliveness.

And then there was my mom's voice, calling my name. CeCe had told my mom that something was wrong. And my mom was there, racing to the junkyard to find me. Everything had been confused and jumbled, with Nathaniel giving Peter his sweater even though they were both soaked with rain, and Nathaniel trying to explain what had happened to my mom. But all I really saw, or remember, was my mom running toward me and sweeping me up in a tight hug.

She brought us all back to our house, and then called Peter's dad, and then, when Peter asked, Ms. Shay.

Uncle Ray wrapped us all in tight blankets, and brought out sweet potato blondies, which were the strangest snack I've ever had because 1) sweet potato and 2) I really liked them. Peter took one too, but just played with it in his hands.

"I'm sorry," Peter said after a long moment, staring at the living room rug.

"Thanks," I said, and when he finally met my gaze, I held it. "That means a lot."

"Yeah," Nathaniel said. "It does. And I'm sorry too, Pete."

Peter nodded, and gave Nathaniel a shaky smile.

"Are . . . are you okay?" I asked after a minute, after

Peter and Nathaniel had both blown their noses. "I mean, can we help?"

"It'll be okay, I think," Peter said. And then, haltingly, he told us about his parents' divorce. They'd been fighting a lot—that's why Peter was always talking to Ms. Shay. He told us how guilty he'd felt because he wanted to go live with his mom, but worried what would happen to his dad if he did.

Soon after, Peter's dad came to get him. But Ms. Shay was there too, and they all agreed to go to Peter's house and talk. The next morning, Nathaniel heard from his parents—who were still friends with Peter's mom—that he'd be going to live with her for a while.

And after spending the school year hating Peter, it was funny to realize that all I wanted were good things for him. I hoped he'd be okay.

Nathaniel's parents took him home soon after, and I was left to be fussed over.

And in all the calls and adults parading in and out, I hadn't had a chance to tell Nathaniel what I'd seen, just as we left the clearing in the junkyard. I saw—

"Mo, it's time for a checkup," CeCe said, interrupting my thoughts and brandishing her plastic stethoscope.

Serenity squeaked in protest, but didn't growl, which was huge.

"Okay, Dr. CeCe," I said. I wrapped her in a tight hug. "You're the best."

"I told you I'm a good helper," CeCe said, nudging me away so she could "listen" to my heart. "I've had lots of practice too," she said matter-of-factly, as she moved the stethoscope to "listen" to my forehead. "I put you to bed at night when you walk."

"Wait, what?" I asked, doing a double take, and almost whacking my head into the plastic stethoscope toy.

"You've been sleepwalking again?!" my mom said from the easy chair. She put down her crossword, looking shocked. "Why didn't you tell me?!"

"Well, I didn't want to worry you," I said.

"Mom doesn't have to worry," CeCe added. "I've been taking care of you. I make you sit down, and then I put a blanket or pillow on you and I sing. Problem solved!"

"Pillow . . . *on* her?" my mom said, after a pause.

"That explains a lot," I said.

I pulled CeCe into another hug, and she hugged me back (but then also took the opportunity to "listen" to the back of my head with the toy stethoscope).

And I realized that CeCe didn't want or need me to

protect her from every bruise or keep her from every fall. She'd been trying to tell me that all this time. But I'd been so distracted by keeping her safe, I hadn't listened. I hadn't seen the real CeCe.

Maybe my mom hadn't been seeing the real me either, I realized. She'd been working so hard, the best way she knew how.

Suddenly, I could relate to my mom a little more.

Which was a nice feeling.

I lay down again, and after a little while, closed my eyes. I thought about what I'd seen in the junkyard, just after the storm, as my mom ushered us home. As we were walking away, my mom's arm over my shoulder, something caught my eye, against the trees by the fence. A white shape, bright and gleaming, watched us, her tail wagging. The white dog let out one fierce, joyful bark.

Then she disappeared between the trees.

The memory of that sound played in my head like a song. And the motions of the house and my family swirled around me, unexpected and everyday, and imperfect and perfect all at once.

And maybe that's how I knew, as I drifted off on the couch, that there, held in that moment, between my family new and old, I was really and truly safe.

CHAPTER 28

SOFT SOIL

Here's a memory. If you were going to set it to a
tune, I'd recommend "Changes" by David Bowie.
Or, for a less literal soundtrack, "Born to Run" by Bruce
Springsteen.

It happened last week, the first week of summer
vacation, when Laura came to visit.

We had, if you can believe it, a *bonfire* in Uncle Ray's
backyard. Laura, my mom, Uncle Ray, CeCe, Auntie
Carol, Nathaniel, and Kerissa were there, and I held a
marshmallow on a stick *directly* over the fire and toasted
s'mores, which I think is probably the bravest thing I've
ever done. Of course, I also had a fire extinguisher right
next to me, just in case.

I am what I am.

Before she left for the night, Auntie Carol took my
hand.

"You seem better," she said.

"I am," I said.

"I'm glad," she said. "You're a wonderful, strong
girl, and you deserve some easier times. Make sure

Uncle Ray and your mom take good care of you, okay?"

"I will." I smiled.

Laura and I talked almost all night long, and I said I was sorry for avoiding her this year, and she said she was sorry, that she just never knew what to say. And we talked, and laughed, and gossiped, and she convinced me to ask Kerissa to the Fall Dance next year (she promised to coach me on the phone, to help me summon up the courage).

And we promised that next year, we'd visit as much as we could.

It was the best visit. And I got to relive it all again when I told the story to Dr. B later that week.

She's my new therapist. Ms. Shay recommended her.

My mom has one too. And Mom sat me down, a few nights ago, and explained all about how sad she's been feeling these past few months, and how she's now taking medication to help her brain produce the chemicals it needs to help with her depression. She told me how sorry she is for not realizing she needed help sooner. Together, my mom and I walked through that door that we'd first opened with angry words. But this time, we did it with understanding, and explanations, and *I'm sorry*s and *I love you*s on all sides.

Dr. B is helping me to see that even if my mind

feels that danger is near, that doesn't mean it's true, but it also doesn't mean I'm silly. She says that feeling anxious and scared and unsafe is one way humans deal with loss. And she says that that's what happened with S-Dad: a real, true, painful loss that I'm entitled to feel every single way about. And best of all, she never tells me "just relax." She says the key is to be aware of your fears, and not to let those fears control your life.

Because fear may always be a part of you. And that's okay. You can still dance forward, even when it's there.

I thought about Dr. B's words when S-Dad came back to the East Coast for work a few weeks later. He took CeCe for the afternoon.

He still didn't talk to me, other than wave through the window.

It still makes me sad and mad.

But then Uncle Ray was sitting in his music room, waiting for me. I sat in the chair next to him. Without saying anything, he put a record on high.

We both sang and screamed our hearts out.

When S-Dad left, I felt like the ground under my feet had disappeared, like disaster had engulfed me, and no one cared. It was hard not to feel like I had to bury my feelings down and forget them, covering over the debris like a junkyard, building a house and a life on top of them, and trying my best to forget they were there.

Only I guess things come up in the soft soil.

That, I hadn't expected.

And as Serenity leapt on my lap and wagged his tail to the beat, I remembered that families don't just break and burn.

Sometimes they grow.

Sometimes, buried in unexpected places, you find new ones.

Nathaniel and I sat in Uncle Ray's backyard, looking out over the woods. It'd been a busy summer. Just that morning, we'd helped Uncle Ray and Lavender—they've started a committee to advocate for Lavender's museum idea, and we were making posters and flyers for their first meeting. We already had a bunch of people who were interested in coming, and the first one had been, if you can believe it, Unofficial Tour Guide (whose real name is Dave, but let's be honest—he'll always be Unofficial Tour Guide to me).

"You know," Nathaniel said quietly, looking out into the distance, "my parents said my Zayde would be proud. They said I was just like him: helping people, and being there for them when they needed it."

"They're right," I said gently. "He would be proud. I know it."

Nathaniel smiled, and he looked so happy, so much lighter. It was impossible not to smile back.

We sat in silence for a few minutes, staring out at the trees, now blooming, over the junkyard fence.

"Do you still think she's out there?" I asked. He knew who I was talking about.

"Maybe," he said, after a moment's thought. "It's a nice idea."

"Was what we saw real?" I asked finally, looking over at Nathaniel.

"I don't know," he said with a small sigh. "Maybe the world's more complicated than I thought." He looked at his hands. "You know . . . I'm not sure if I want to look for any more ghosts right now . . ."

"Oh, Nathaniel, I—" I began, feeling like I had to make something better.

"But vampires, have you thought about vampires?!" he said, looking at me, eyes bright with interest. "They could be anywhere."

"Or anyone!" I added excitedly.

"Mo, Nathaniel," my mom called from porch. "I'm headed to town, who wants ice cream?"

"Oh, me, me!" we called in chorus, leaping to our feet.

We walked toward the car, debating garlic versus salt as the most effective way to keep vampires away. CeCe came dancing out of the house with a variety of stuffed animals in an old backpack, singing about ice cream, and Uncle Ray followed with a new CD to play in the car.

Just before I got in, I turned back to look at the gnarled old tree, and the junkyard just beyond it. I wondered what had been real. I wondered if there had ever been a ghost in the junkyard.

But I knew one thing for certain.

It didn't feel dangerous anymore.

I smiled and waved goodbye.

EPILOGUE

If Mo had turned around and looked through the rear window as the car drove down the road, she might have seen a big white dog, watching from the woods. She might have seen that the dog was muddy and panting and very much alive, with a collar that had Mrs. Smith's address etched on it in capital letters.

Mo might have seen the dog woof happily, wag her tail, and turn to her own best friend: the largest, shimmering, silvery gray not-dog she'd ever seen.

Mo might have seen the dog and the elephant—who shone translucent and pale in the sun—watch as their car disappeared down the road.

But Mo didn't turn around.

So we don't know for sure.

But maybe, as the two human friends zoomed down the road, the two animal friends turned and made their way into the bramble, all of them off to their next adventure.

ACKNOWLEDGMENTS

This story found its start in many different places. First, thank you to my uncle, Ethan, who insisted I watch the *Springsteen on Broadway* Netflix special with him. Sharing music and stories with you gave me the spark of the idea that became this book.

For a writer, there is the story we tell and the story that gets us to a place where we're ready to tell it. For me, the story that got me here was made possible by Dr. Christopher Bullock, the first therapist who I confessed my fears to, and the person who listened, who told me it was okay and real, and who helped me realize that my life could be more than my anxiety. Even as he faced his own struggles with cancer, Dr. Bullock was there for me in a way that has profoundly shaped my adult life, and it's an honor to dedicate this book to his memory.

Thank you too to Donna Freitas, who gave my new story idea its essential ingredient—voice—by giving me a writing exercise on a train and insisting we write in silence for an hour so she could meet a deadline. The voice I uncovered in that exercise brought me back to the closet-bedroom of my childhood and set Mo on her journey.

There are so many others who made this book what it is. My mom, who has modeled courage, tenacity, and care all my life. My dad, who is for real an aging Chinese hippie and who provides the warp and weft for Uncle Ray. My sisters, Catherine and Sarah, who let me talk through story tangles with them at any hour, encourage me at every turn, and talk in silly voices with me at the drop of a hat. I'm so lucky to be a part of this trio of sisters.

My grandmother got to hear about this story before she passed away, and her memory, humor, and grit shape me and my work at every turn. My grandfather Bobby tells the best jokes (except the chili one) and always supports me (and reminds me to demand my worth and get paid!).

Thank you to Auntie Esther, Uncle Paul, Jenn, Mike, Yvonne, Paul, Kimmy, Jeff—whose love I feel even when a pandemic separates us. And Noah, Ezra, Jeremy, Rachel, Ellie, and Emmett—who remind me to wonder and find fun wherever I go. And, of course, to Martina for teaching me about putting grapes in the freezer: This is now my favorite writing snack.

Thank you, Yanie, the best of friends and writing partners, whose brilliant and caring teaching formed the basis for Lavender. Becky, my support and center in Boston, who always hears my ideas when they're just jumbled sentences and always believes in their potential. Ashley, one of the very first readers of *Toast*, who saw it in its rawest form (and ergo me in my rawest form) and offers unending love and support. Hannah, whose love, thoughtfulness, and professional fierceness are awe-inspiring. Debbi, an amazing friend and inspiring writer who introduced me to Highlights, where writing magic happens. Thank you to Eli, for all those stories we created on our walks to school: the magician 100 percent has a house in New Warren! Thank you too to so many others in my community: Kate, Sarah H., Valerie, Louise, to name just a few, and my UMass Boston colleagues and students.

Unending thanks to Connie Hsu, my incredible editor, who believed in this story from its earliest moments and who has made it better at every revision with deep insight and care. Thank you to Megan Abbate and Nicolàs Ore-Giron for your incredible work helping this book take form. Thank you too to my wonderful agent, Dan Lazar, who is unfailing champion of my work, and to Torie Doherty-Munroe.

Thanks to Cornelia Li for the gorgeous cover, which captures Mo and Maudie in such beauty.

Thank you to Mary Van Akin, Mallory Grigg, Sarah Gompper, Jie Yang, Jen Healey, and all the team at Macmillan.

Thank you to my music readers, the wonderful Joe Jiang and Paula Lee. Getting to meet you and connect over your knowledge of music has been an absolute joy, and I'm so honored to have had your help on this manuscript!

Thank you too to Bruce and Sue: our chance meeting in New Orleans had such an impact on me, and your warmth, kindness, and hearing about your lives in music had a profound role in shaping this story.

And, of course, I couldn't end these acknowledgments without thanking Bruce Springsteen, whose music fueled this entire book, and all the other musicians and artists whose songs take us to other places.

Finally and most of all, to my readers, and anyone out there who sees themselves in Mo: When I was a kid, I worried a lot. As an adult, I worry a lot too. It took me a long time to realize I could talk about these worries. It took me even longer before I could give these worries a name and start to face my anxiety head-on.

If you worry, please know you can talk to someone. If you worry, please know it's okay. And if you worry, please know that you can dance on anyway.

There is wonderful music to life. I can't wait to hear yours.